FALLEN ANGELS: LOGAN

LAW ANGEL

FALLEN ANGELS AND DEMONS
BOOK ONE

ANNA LORES

Blooming Cactus Publishing, LLC

ALSO BY ANNA LORES

Contemporary Romance

Billionaire 42 (Streaming Lovers series) Book 1

Billionaire 43 (Streaming Lovers series), Book 2

Billionaire 44 (Streaming Lovers series), Book 3

Billionaire 45 (Streaming Lovers series), Book 4

Ella's Triple Pleasure (Sinfully Hers series), Book 1

Evangeline's Power Trio (Sinfully Hers series), Book 2

The Horse List, Book 1

The Horse List Challenge, Book 2

The Horse List Unveiled, Book 3

Unexpected Love: Chase Allen

More coming soon

Contemporary Romance Short (er) Stories

Blade's Fertile Virgin, Book 1

Stetson's Fertile Virgin, Book 2

Greg's Fertile Virgin, Book 3

Evan's Fertile Virgin, Book 4

Brandon's Fertile Virgin, Book 5

Maverick's Fertile Virgin, Book 6

Denver's Fertile Virgin, Book 7

Bastian's Fertile Virgin, Book 8

Quinn's Fertile Virgin, Book 9

Malcolm's Fertile Virgin, Book 10

Brianna's Fertile Virgin, Book 11

Blade's Second Fertile Virgin, Book 12

Nash's Fertile Virgin, Book 13 is coming soon…

Paranormal Romance

Werewolves and Vampires

Cursed to Love

One Night of Love

More coming soon

Fallen Angels and Demons Series

Fallen Angels: Logan, Book 1

Fallen Angels: Slater, Book 2 will be coming soon

More coming soon

For more steamy stories and to join Anna's VIP Lounge, visit https://www.AnnaLoresAuthor.com

CONTENTS

This book is a work of fiction. While reference might be made to actual historical events or existing locations, the names, characters, places and incidents are either the product of the author's imagination or are used fictitiously, and any resemblance to actual persons, living or dead, business establishments, events, or locales is entirely coincidental.

Warning

This print or e-book contains sexually explicit scenes and adult language and may be considered offensive to some readers. The spicy division of Blooming Cactus Publishing, LLC's print and e-books are for sale to adults ONLY, as defined by the laws of the country in which you made your purchase. Please store your files wisely, where they cannot be accessed by under-aged readers.

DISCLAIMER: *Please do not try any new sexual practice, without the guidance of an experienced practitioner. Neither Blooming Cactus Publishing LLC nor its authors will be responsible for any loss, harm, injury or death resulting from use of the information contained in any of its titles.*

ACKNOWLEDGMENTS

Thank you for buying this book. I know your time is sacred, so thank you for choosing to spend it reading Logan and Aurora's story.

I wrote most of these books while I was in the throws of colon cancer and trying to beat it. There are references to God in this book and very little cursing in the series. I thought a lot about angels and demons while undergoing treatments for cancer. I thought about the fight for souls, and five stories came to me during that time for this series. It's a little different than my other novels, but it's sexy and sweet, and there remains an undercurrent of darkness that the characters struggle with in different ways.

Whatever you may be struggling with, I want you to know that I love you. And if you'd like me to pray for you, I will. Email me at Anna@annaloresauthor.com. I know many of you prayed for me while I was dealing with colon cancer. Let me tell you, I felt those prayers. Thank you for them.

As a reminder…The age for colon cancer screening is 45 — please get screened for colon cancer. It truly could save your life. I love you and I want you to live. And tell those you love and care about to get screened.

To my family, thanks for all the love and support

you've given me. I love you all more than I am able to express.

To Sarah Marek and Benjamin Moder, the amazing artists who designed the cover...I'm so happy to have you in my life, and I love you dearly. Thank you for your beautiful work on this cover.

A special thanks to my editor Dianne Rich for all the prayers and support. Thank you for polishing Logan and Aurora's world. Thank you for being a friend. Thank you for working with me when my world turned upside down. Thank you. :)

To: Amiee W.

"…*When the wicked perish, the righteous thrive.*"
-Proverbs 28:28

CHAPTER ONE

Aurora

Stepping out of the car onto a gravel drive, Aurora Smith stared at the freshly-painted white two-bedroom farmhouse where her father's only real friend Logan Hutchison lived. She should've been thankful the man was willing to take her in and give her a place to live, after all these years without any contact from her father or mother, and she was.

But the fact that he couldn't fly to Atlanta and travel with her to his ranch when he was contacted seemed all too telling of his real feelings about the situation. The man didn't want her here. She couldn't blame him for not wanting her. Why would any single man want a teen orphan who was in hiding from a murdering psychopath?

Honestly, she was surprised her mom wrote Logan down as an emergency contact in the first place. Aurora hadn't seen him since she was seven. She'd been in the height of her awkward phase. She was still awkward. Awkward and scared and turned eighteen today. Not that she told him that today was her birthday. She didn't. The subject didn't come up when he called and told her he'd probably get home close to the time she'd be arriving at his ranch.

Today should've been so different than the reality she was facing. While she drove the last leg of the journey from Georgia to Texas, she'd found herself pulling over to the side of the road to "manage her feelings" as if there was a way to manage something so uncontrollable...so horrific...so life-altering. Emotions ran Aurora's life as much as they ran her mother's. Once control was lost for either of them, everyone within a twenty-mile radius felt their presence. She had to keep her emotions in check or he'd know she was different. That she was weird. That she could do things no one else could do.

So much hung in the balance for her today. She needed Logan to keep her safely tucked away on his ranch. He was the only person Mom trusted. And if her mom trusted him, then she did, too.

She thought, *if he takes one look at me and decides I'm too much trouble, I'm screwed. I'll be homeless. I'll be...lost or dead or worse—taken by the man who murdered my parents.*

Logan, please take me in for more than a week. I'll do anything you want. I know you can protect me, or Mom wouldn't have written you down as an emergency contact. Please keep me safe and let me stay at least until I've figured out how to protect myself.

At the moment, she had no plans and no idea what to do without her mom. When she lost her mother, she lost her best friend, her lifeline, her protector. She'd loved her father, but she'd depended on her mother.

The front porch screen door swung open and a tall guy with wavy, light-brown hair wearing dark jeans and a blue T-shirt stepped out.

You can't be Logan. You're gorgeous. Who are you?

"Is that you, Aurora?" the man asked.

With her hand ready to either open the car door wide or close it behind her, climb back into the seat of the beater compact, and hightail it out of there, she cocked her head to the right and lurched forward, trying to get a better look at the man. Surely, the man on the porch couldn't be the same Logan Hutchison that her dad stayed in semi-touch with from his hometown. The same guy who had gifted her dad a car—a car he lost in the same poker game he won the crappy one she'd driven here in. It was a surprise that the old thing passed inspection, but it did. Every time. But the car didn't have much more life in it. Truthfully, she was surprised that the clunker made the trip all the way here. But it did, and she was thankful.

"Yes, sir. It's me, *Mr. Hutchison?*"

I hope you're the Logan Hutchison who my parents trusted, but you look too young to be him. You don't look that much older than me. Dang, the light around you is breathtakingly ethereal. I've never seen anything like it.

Narrowing her focus from the beauty of the golden ribbons expanding from his mesmerizing white aura, she took a step forward, attempting to catch more than a glimpse of the brown-haired man on the porch through the expanding bright colors of his spirit.

You're different. You're special. There's no darkness inside you.

You're not like my father. And you're nothing like the man who took my parents from me.

"Yep, it's me. Call me Logan." He waved.

"Where should I park?" She squinted, trying to see beyond the brilliance of his aura, which had already spread across the land as far as her eyes could see.

Exhaling, she thought of the facts about the man her parents had told her about most of her life. *I know you're younger than Dad by at least five or six years—possibly more, and Dad and Mom had me when they were sixteen. So you'd be at the oldest twenty-nine, but could be younger. Dang, you look much younger…How could you look so young?*

"You're fine parked right where you are." He bent over and pulled on his brown cowboy boots, details of his appearance slowly filtering through the purity of his spiritual light. As he hustled down the steps, moving closer toward her, his aura expanded in every direction. The brilliance of the white light all around softened the nearer he came, allowing her to see more and more of the strong and sexy man who invited her into his home.

Oh Lord, I'm thinking of him as sexy. He is sexy. I'm actually attracted to him. I'd marry him. Lord, what is wrong with me?

He stopped in front of her as she closed the car door behind her. "Where's all your stuff?"

Speechless, she stared into his ethereal ice-blue eyes. *Oh my goodness, you're the most gorgeous man I've ever seen in my life. You're not going to want me to stay and screw up your dating life. I want to be the one you want to date. I want to…I'm so stupid. I can't have fantasies of love and happy endings with you. You're gonna want me out of your house and off your property as soon as possible.*

She slipped her backpack off her shoulder and held it up. "This is all that was left."

She'd never had much. Dad always said that if all a person's stuff didn't fit in a backpack, then they had too much. Because of Dad's gambling, living as if they were fugitives came in handy more times than not. But this time, the backpack and items in it were donations from the principal at her high school. The only pictures left of her life were on her phone, and her father had deleted most of them in his *weekly purge of unnecessary things*. Dad always said that she needed to *live in the moment, not the past*. But she liked having memories of good times, probably because they were few and far between.

"Yeah, yeah. Sorry," Logan said. "It was a stupid question. We'll get you what you need tomorrow. The important thing is that you're here and safe." In an effort to take her backpack, his calloused fingertips brushed across the back of her hand.

A spark of electricity instantly permeated her flesh and travelled straight to her belly, morphing into fiery lust. That intense desire hit her so hard that it dove downward into parts that had never been touched or awakened prior to that moment.

Halting for an instant, he gazed at her and then seemed to shake off whatever he was thinking. While she attempted to douse the fire inside her from creeping to the surface, he took her backpack and slung it over his shoulder. He carried it to the porch, took off his boots, and placed them beside the door on a mat.

"Welcome to The Hutchison Ranch. It's been in the family for centuries." He glanced at her flip-flops—

another donation from her principal. "We'll get you a good pair of boots tomorrow."

"Thanks for helping me out, Mr. Hutchison." She stood dwarfed next to him. The man was built like a Viking—tall and broad. But with a royal influence that gave him a perfectly proportioned face that wasn't too hard or too soft, and his motions seemed effortless, as if he walked on air, almost floating along an air current of his own. He moved like a majestic bird flying in the sky, beautiful, powerful, and deadly, if necessary.

"Please, call me Logan." His voice vibrated through her bones like a cozy caress, promising so much more. "My home has always been open to you. I'm glad the police called and that you answered your phone when I…" He lowered his gaze. "Anyway, this is your home now."

He opened the second door down the hall just past the living room. "I emptied out the dresser and closet. I hope the bed is okay. I bought it yesterday, and, well, you can paint the room or keep it dove-white. It's yours to decorate however you want. Think about it tonight. Tomorrow, we'll go into town to shop, and I'll show you around." He strode inside without making a sound and placed her backpack on the beautiful, pastel-pink quilt that reminded her of the one her mom had made her when she'd turned sixteen.

"You didn't have to do all this," Aurora said.

"I need to do more," he mumbled. He skimmed his hand over the quilt and turned around. "Do you need pajamas or…"

"Not tonight. My principal gave me a few things for the trip and has sent in my application and transcripts to the private college here for possible acceptance for enrollment for the fall. They allowed my high school grades to stand and gave me my diploma early, so I wouldn't have to come back next month for a ceremony that I probably wouldn't have attended anyway. Now, I'm a high school graduate as of two days ago."

"That was nice that they—"

She shrugged. "Yeah. They gave me gas money to get here, too. They were better to me than they needed to be. It's just..." The words she hadn't planned to speak aloud worked their way out. "If I hadn't spent the night working, I would've been at the apartment studying. I might have been able to save—"

Logan pulled her into a big hug. "Don't do that to yourself. It's not your fault. None of what happened is your fault."

With his arms around her, all the strength and stoicism and semi-denial she'd managed to hold onto for the last few days fled. She wrapped her arms around the handsome stranger and held onto him for dear life.

"I've got you, sweetie. You've got nothing to fear here. No one comes out this way unless they're coming to see me or my neighbors, Malcolm and Ranger Wentworth. The Wentworths don't invite strangers to visit their ranch. This part of town is too far off the beaten path for even a directionally-challenged driver to show up lost."

She nodded, believing him. But the tide of emotions she'd squelched for far too long rose to the surface, and she couldn't hold back the sobs anymore. The damn broke and tears rushed down her cheeks. She hated it, but the more she tried to control her emotions from total release, the more the recent memories of the crime scene filled her mind, pushing her to either retreat or lose total control. "I don't want to go back to Atlanta."

"If it comes down to your presence being needed in court to prosecute the…" He didn't say the word. "Aurora, we'll go together." He rubbed her back, and that small gesture gave her comfort. "I'm sorry you had to drive yourself here. If I hadn't been out of town dealing with a church emergency myself, I would have been there for you."

He squeezed her tighter, holding her together from scattering into a billion pieces of uncontrolled emotions. If she lost control, an emotional beacon would alert all sorts of evil entities that she was here and vulnerable. Then the man would come and take her. Take her and torture her, kill her like he did her parents.

"Don't you worry about anything," Logan said. "This is your home now, and I won't let anything bad happen to you."

Aurora's breathing hitched with each intake of oxygen, but she began gluing each outlying emotion together again, mentally pulling the strewn puzzle pieces of her powers closer, to balance her feelings and gain strength to keep going on God's path, wherever it led.

"I've got to feed my dogs and put the horses in the barn before it gets dark," he said. "There's dinner in the crockpot. You can wait for me to finish, or eat now. You're gonna hear some barking and animal sounds you might not recognize. Don't fret. If you get scared, call my cell. If I don't answer, call me again and again, until I do. Sometimes, I don't hear the phone when I'm working. And you can always come and get me. But grab a pair of my boots from my closet and put them on before you go chasing after me. We're in rattlesnake country."

"Yes, sir." She took in a deep breath and didn't want to let him go, preferring to stay in his embrace. Hanging onto him and the safety and comfort he provided wouldn't last. Like everything in her life, he was a temporary solution.

She stepped back, and her hands dropped to her sides. She was alone again, even though he remained inches from her. Growing up like a nomad, moving from place to place, had forced her to get used to letting people and things go, no matter how much it hurt.

"We will share a bathroom until I do some more renovations. Sorry. It's a small house. Just keep the doors closed and knock before you go in, and I'll do the same. I'm making an addition onto the house with my grandfather's help, but it is slow going. Oh, and there's a half-bath off the kitchen that I recently added that you can use, too."

"Thanks." The house was bigger than she expected. Actually, the place seemed like a mansion from the inside, and didn't need an addition. The front of the house didn't represent the inside. Each room she walked through was double and triple the normal size of the rooms she was used to. And the ceilings...twenty and thirty feet high in most of the rooms, except for the guest bedroom...her bedroom.

She held her hand to her heart. *You prepared a room for me. My own room. In your house.* She hadn't had her own separate space in years.

She lowered her gaze to the polished wooden floor. *Did*

you install the flooring? Did you do all the renovations yourself? Dad used to say you could build anything.

He seemed to hesitate as he stepped back, adding more distance between them. But his hesitation could've been in her mind. She wasn't sure. The fantasy of being his wife flashed through her mind. She wished he would step forward again and hold her, maybe even kiss her. The desire filled every molecule in her system. The feeling was so strong that she did something that was out of character for her. She stepped forward, raised onto her tippy toes, and kissed his cheek. The spark that accompanied his touch earlier happened again, only it lingered longer within her and made her lips tingle with heat.

He didn't move, but he closed his eyes for a moment. Only a moment. When his gaze met hers, his blue eyes had slivers of gold that hadn't been there seconds earlier. And in a blink of an eye, those slivers of gold vanished. Maybe she imagined the change in his eyes.

She stepped back, even though she wanted to curl her arms around him and never let go. *I need to get a grip. Keep a polite distance. Don't get too close.*

"Um, I'll wait until your chores are finished and eat dinner with you." She touched her fingers to her tingling lips and turned away from him, afraid of what she might do if he were to show any interest at all in her. "I'm going to wash up while you're working."

"I'll be back as quickly as I can," he said.

The only sound she heard from his retreat was the door to the bedroom closing, and even that was almost inaudible.

Closing her eyes, she basked in the energy he'd left in

the room. *No wonder Mom trusted him. He's different. He's pure. He's perfect.*

CHAPTER TWO

Aurora

Alone in his house, Aurora walked into the bathroom. When she saw the door to his bedroom stood wide open, her curiosity got the better of her. She moved closer and peeked into his room.

Thick, twisted, rugged steel poles connected by fine metal wires formed a masterfully made headboard depicting a creative scene of running horses woven through it. A simple dark chocolate blanket over cream sheets made up the bed. Two cream-colored pillows lay flat at the top of the bed beneath the horses as if the steeds were racing on the beach. Two smaller spiraling spindles formed the corners of the footboard with simple metal wires braided together connecting the two metal spindles. A six-drawer dresser made of beautifully crafted wood with the sides, corners, and front formed with similar spiral metal accents to match the bed was the only other piece of furniture in the room. Seven moving boxes sat in the southern corner of the room near the door to what had to have been a closet.

Are those boxes the things you took out of the guest room? Or are they from your military service? Part of your position in your church? Are they filled with family memories? How long have you lived here?

There were so many questions that she'd probably never ask. So many things about his life that she wanted to know.

As she closed the door to his room, she turned her attention to the bathroom. The white porcelain soaking tub sparkled like new. The polished nickel faucet and body sprayer shined. The faint scent of caulk and bleach lingered, holding enough of an aroma that she searched for the finishing touches of a recent installation of a toilet which sat farther away from the tub in the open space. Logan Hutchison had definitely spent some time today in that bathroom making sure she had the basics of a home finished.

Maybe you'll let me stay for a while. I want to stay. I want to stay for a long, long time. I don't think I ever want to leave.

In the small renovated space, the design allowed room for two people to walk comfortably together from one door to the other. A married couple and a child could easily share the bathroom, working around each other as they got ready for the day.

The white vanity cabinets and mirror spread across the length of the wall between the rooms. The white and silver granite counter and two sinks matched the floor tile. White drawers and cabinets filled out the base while a huge mirror rose from the granite counter to the incredibly high ceiling with recessed lighting above. A heated towel rack with white towels folded over the four bars was attached to the wall nearest the door leading to the guest room where she was staying.

Curiosity led her to search through the cabinets, finding everything from shampoo to toothbrushes to razors and first aid kits. She felt bad for snooping, but not bad enough that it would plague her for more than a few minutes. She kept repeating to herself that she didn't know the man. And even with his bright and honest aura and the spark of life and warmth from his touch, along with the instinctive trust she had in him—enough to have a melt-down as soon as he hugged her—she still had to remain diligent in looking for any signs he might have addictive, darkness-seeking tendencies like her father.

Vigilance in searching for the dangers in the people around her remained her top priority. She kept physical contact with people to a minimum, even while working. From a young age, her mom warned her of the dangers of getting too close to people. She'd seen Dad move from person to person without anyone ever stopping him. But when Mom stepped within arm's reach of a person, that person would grab her, need to touch her, and wouldn't let go without force. Everyone, men and women alike, wanted time with her mom.

As Aurora grew up, she realized she'd inherited whatever bad mojo her mom had that made people addicted to her. People began trying to touch her, and once they had, they didn't want to stop until someone else made them or she found a way to escape their strong grip. When stalkers appeared at the door to their apartment, Aurora and her family knew it was time to move, to hide.

She'd never forget the moment she realized just how different she and her mom were from other women. She was ten and a pair of Dad's friends tried to kidnap her. The couple had such evil inside them that Aurora screamed and screamed and screamed to get away. The more Aurora screamed, the tighter they held her, squeezing the air from her lungs. The darkness the couple carried circled Aurora like ropes constricting her arms and legs, her chest. Oxygen hovered over her mouth, but the darkness blocked its entrance. The longer they held her, the more the darkness closed in, suffocating her physically and spiritually. But the light of her aura continued to shine, refusing to give in to the darkness.

The couple had hit her. They tried to kill her. But her dad came to the rescue, ripping her from their crushing arms before they could snuff the life force from her. With her in his arms, he ran out of the apartment as she clung to him with what little strength she had left. He ran so fast and so far, carrying her through streets and alleys as the couple chased him. In her eyes, he was the strongest man in the entire world as he sprinted through alleys and streets. He leapt over fences and raced through buildings to lose them, which he eventually did.

Her father was the most formidable man she knew, even with the never-ending stream of darkness flowing like a river within him, haunting him. He was always slowly drowning in the darkness, but he loved her. He loved her mom. But love was never enough. He was an addict, too. The darkness always found a way into his spirit, his heart, his soul. As much as her father fought the evil invading his soul, the darkness always found a way to win…*This world is the devil's domain.*

But Logan seemed different than her father. From what she sensed, Logan might not have any darkness in him. But if he got too close to discovering her secret, he might develop an addiction or…No. If he was dangerous, her mom would never have put him as an emergency contact. She trusted him to be a good man in every aspect of his life.

I need to trust Logan, like my mom trusted him. I need to listen to my instincts. I need to be confident he'll protect me, if those men from Atlanta come looking for me. I need to believe that if he found out about what I could—and would—do under certain circumstances, he'd still protect me. I need to believe that he wouldn't use me like Dad used Mom, and in the end, the way Dad tried to use me.

Inhaling the clean energy that remained strong in the house, she shook out her arms and shut down the bad memories. She rummaged through his drawers, finding a hand towel. She washed her hands and placed the towel on the counter closest to the guest room, hoping that leaving it on the counter would be okay. They hadn't talked about rules, but she planned to watch and follow his lead in everything he did.

The ranch wasn't anything like her home in the city. Living in an apartment in Atlanta, she was used to small quarters. But the apartment didn't seem small to her. Dad was rarely home, so it was just her and her mom most of the time. There was no privacy in the apartment. She heard everything. Now she was in a house where she would have privacy. Yet, she doubted she'd be able to hide anything from Logan. Not that she had anything to hide. She had nothing to hide. Well, that's not exactly true. She did have one thing to hide, but it wasn't a bad secret. It was good, or it could be good, as long as the secret was kept a secret. Her father didn't keep it a secret. He used her mother for her ability. He ended up trying to use Aurora, too, once he realized she'd inherited similar abilities.

Staring at the mirror, she combed her fingers through the lengths of her long, loose, blonde curls. She wondered how long it would take before Logan figured out her secret. How long would she have here before someone noticed she wasn't like everyone else and had to move? How long would she have before the healing power she contained within her spirit would release without her consent? Her mom had more control and tried to teach Aurora some of the lessons her own mother had taught her. But the lessons were few and far between. And now, her mom was gone.

The pain, blood, and tears associated with healing would forever be her burden to bear, never to know her mother's secret of a pain-free healing. She wouldn't be able to hide the physical evidence of healing others. Logan would know any blood that stained her clothes wouldn't be his. That if someone was hurt and she touched them, her blood would flow, not theirs. She'd feel the pain, not them. She'd develop their wounds, and they would heal. When she came to her full power, her blue eyes would turn gold, probably permanently, like her mother's had. Danger and death would search for her like they did her mom. Darkness and death would find her, like they had her mother and grandmother, and her mother before her.

Would Logan take her far away? Lock her up? Use her for financial gain? Or would he protect her like her grandmother's husband had done for her grandmother? Like her father had promised to do for her mother? Would he fail like her father had, sending her mother into the devil's lair again and again? Would Logan introduce her to the devil's demons living in the city, like her father had done to her mother?

I need to hide my abilities as long as possible. No one is like me. No one else has angel blood flowing through their veins. I'm an anomaly in this world. If Dad had just kept his mouth shut about Mom. If he'd just kept away from the darkness in the city. If he'd never mentioned he had a wife and daughter whose ability to heal was unparalleled, then the evil man wouldn't have sought us out. The man's obsession with me would've never begun.

Fear shook her to her core. Her hands trembled, gripping the granite counter, as the memories of the series of her father's mistakes brought her here, to this ranch in Exorcise, Texas. Dad's drinking and gambling took him down a spiraling path into the depth of Satan's dungeon. His inability to keep a job for more than a couple months kept them moving from one place to another.

Mom's constant excuses for him left Aurora wondering how long it would take before her mom became as corrupt as her father. The demons disguised as men that her father brought to the apartment to pay off his gambling debts, used Mom's ability…Their darkness sucked more and more of the light from her mother's spirit each time they visited. The evil clung like tar to the walls and yanked the chains of sin that carried her father further into the devil's snare of addiction.

For some reason, Aurora and her mom were kept from

any evil invading their bodies and souls—at least Aurora thought so before she saw her mom's white aura become murky and then morph into a charcoal gray the weeks leading up to her death. Being constantly surrounded by people doomed to darkness seemed to have taken its toll on her mom's soul. Her mom had whispered to her before bed, more nights than not, that loving a man bound for Hell was the punishment cast onto her from above.

Did you follow Dad down into Hell to try and save him? Or did he pull you down with him to spend eternity in darkness?

Aurora tugged at her curly strands of hair, stretching a handful down to her belly. Her mom would straighten it with a flat iron every morning before they left the apartment for school and work. That flat iron was always in her mom's backpack. That and clear shimmering lip gloss. She was so beautiful, always smiling when Dad came home in a rush and told them they were moving immediately. He led and she followed, taking Aurora's hand and telling her that it was time to start a new adventure.

As a family, they fled, moving from one apartment to another, month after month, year after year. No matter how many times her mom attempted spiritual cleanses with her father, he always harbored that mustard seed of darkness deep inside him. And that seed always sprouted when their lives began to move in a positive direction. The sprout of darkness always lured him back into the shadows, turning the small sprig to a full blown, mature tree that needed to be chopped down. And she and her mother tried chopping it down, grinding it up and burying it, allowing him a glimpse of light, sometimes even propelling him to step into a bath of purity for a day or two or even a few weeks but never longer.

As Aurora grew up, she joined her mother in the purifying rituals, but those didn't chase away the darkness forever, not from her father. The rituals did help the neighborhoods. Well, it helped *some* people in the neighborhoods where they lived. Those who hadn't already sold their souls to the devil, found a way to get out from under evil's oppression.

The spiritual light she and her mother sent out became a path for those ready to walk toward God's plan for their lives. Most didn't take it. Most were swallowed up into the darkness.

As Mom's light and powers waned over the years, her spirit darkened. She became too weak to attempt a cleansing ritual alone or with Aurora. She counted on Aurora to continue the work, and Aurora did what she could, but it wasn't enough. They needed another angel to complete the spiritual cleansing rituals, but they hadn't come across another angel. Not just any angel would do, either. Aurora needed the strength of an angel whose body and spirit were pure. An angel whose presence gave her the strength to bond and pour light and goodness into the world, to balance the power of good and evil. An angel who could possibly shift the scales so that good would have an advantage over evil. An angel who fought evil and won. An angel who fought for justice. An angel who could've saved her parents from the nightmare that became their death...*The room covered in blood and darkness. The man with a soul blacker than night. The acrid scent of death and decay...*

Struggling to breathe through the memories, Aurora placed her trembling hands, palms down, on the smooth granite counter.

Inhale goodness. Exhale fear. Breathe in life. Release worry.

Nothing she did stopped the tide of anxiety rushing toward her, vomiting the naïve choices she made that inevitably brought her here to Texas.

Maybe she shouldn't have taken that job as a waitress at the local sports bar and grill to try and get enough money to help her parents move away from the city, permanently. Maybe she shouldn't have told her father about the job and her plans to help financially. Maybe then he wouldn't have told the man who demanded to meet her about her job. Maybe the man wouldn't have found her so easily.

She'd been so careful, always wearing the uniform with long-sleeve shirt and pants to cover as much skin as possible, to reduce the likelihood of her powers manifesting to heal a stranger. Maybe the man wouldn't have followed her into the back, when another waitress was assigned his table. Maybe he wouldn't have cornered her near the kitchen and grabbed her hand, starting the chain of events that led to her parents' deaths.

But that first link of the chain started with the touch of his hand, leading to another link added to the chain with the attack outside the restaurant near the patio tables in front of a table filled with police officers. If the man hadn't assaulted her and tried to drag her into the alley, then the police wouldn't have gotten involved. But the man *did* assault her and attempted to kidnap her. And the police *did* get involved adding more and more links to the chain that rattled and rattled. She could still hear the metallic, scraping sound of his voice as he called her name while he was face down on the ground with two officers on top of him.

The cops assured her that the man would leave her alone after a little time in jail. But the man didn't leave her alone, not while he was in jail, or when he got out. The restraining orders didn't stop him from coming after her. Nothing stopped him. Not the arrests. Not the stints in jail after each public assault. Not the silence on her end. Not the bouncers at her job. Not even moving to another cash-only apartment stopped him. The man always found where she lived and worked. And her father led him to her, offering her a new phone number and schedule, time after time after time.

Begging her frantic heart rate to slow, to halt the rush of grief from taking her back to her last apartment, to her last double-shift at work. She had to end this cycle that terrible man had started. But if she were being honest with herself, it was her father who started the cycle ending his own life and her mother's, and nearly hers.

She walked out of the bathroom into the guest room, hoping a change of scenery would stop all the memories from terrorizing her.

She crawled under the covers on the bed. Drawing the quilt up to her chin, she curled in a tight ball as tears flowed down her cheeks. The memories tugged at her until she lost balance and stumbled along the path they led—down a road of destruction...

Nothing stopped the man when he got out of jail this last time. He came for me, and brought friends. Only I wasn't there. I was called in at the last minute to work a double shift. I was working while that piece of shit murdered my parents and burned what few belongings we owned.

She gripped the edge of the quilt, begging for the memories to end. But they continued.

While I walked past the flashing blue lights, up the stairs to the second level of the low-income rental, my heart hammered in my chest, terrified of what I'd find. An officer held me back at the door, but I still saw the crime scene. I saw the bodies. I saw the blood. I saw the darkness snuffing out the remnants of light from the cleansing ritual my mother and I had completed earlier that afternoon. I saw my mother's body emit a dim light and crumble to ash. The ashes rose and floated over my father, then covered him, as if she was trying to protect him, even in death.

And then the soulless eyes of evil met mine. He had waited for me to come home. He'd waited next to my parents' bodies, next to the metal barrel in the living room my dad would start a small fire in to keep warm at night. The man greeted the me as if he were hosting some kind of celebration for the police officers, while he waited for me to arrive.

A cop pushed me behind him as the evil man walked by in handcuffs.

"I did this for you, for us," the man said. "I know what you can do. Your father and mother told me everything. They told me, and now I know exactly what you can do. I know who you are. I'm coming back for you. I'm going to find you wherever you go. I'll search the world for you, Aurora. I'll never stop."

"I'll search the world for you, Aurora," continuously played on repeat in her head. She rocked back and forth, trying to find some kind of comfort as she held her tongue from screaming to make his voice shut up, to force his dark eyes from staring at her.

The man would never stop searching for her. He'd do anything to have her, to touch her, to use her, and to cover her in so much evil she'd turn into one of them.

She needed a protector. She needed someone who was stronger than her father, much stronger. She needed a man who wouldn't succumb to any of the deals the devil would offer him. She needed a man who was so good and pure that darkness would flee from his presence.

She prayed that Logan would be that man. That he'd never leave her. That he'd never make her go back to that place and face that man alone.

CHAPTER THREE

Logan

"Aurora?" He didn't want to scare her, but the colors of her aura had expanded inside the house. The energy shifted around her. The gray and brown hues fought against the stark white of her spirit. The colors separated and swarmed against the white, tangling and swirling around in utter chaos. The girl had been through enough. Now she battled in her sleep. She should be resting, finding peace in her dreams. He'd told her there was nothing to fear. He'd promised to protect her. His home, his land, his people remained safe, yet she tossed and turned in her bed fighting off someone or something. He lived to protect his people and territory, to uphold the laws of the church and follow God's orders.

What sparked your nightmares, Aurora? You were fine when I left. Are you thinking about your parents? Are you thinking about the court hearing? About going back there? I'll be with you.

He pressed his ear to her bedroom door. The sound of sheets rustling grew louder. *Are you running away? Still fighting?*

"Aurora?" he whispered. "Are you okay?"

Whimpers filtered through the door and the energy that expanded from the room felt like knives entering his heart.

I need to help you. You've been fighting demons your whole life, and probably have no idea what you've been up against.

"I'm coming in to check on you," he said.

Please, don't be naked. I don't need to be any more attracted to you than I already am. I want to wrap my fingers around your blonde-hair. I bet it's as silky as feathers from an angel's wings.

A quick turn of the glass doorknob and he gently pushed the door open.

The cascading moonlight streamed through the window across from him, spotlighting her small body curled in a fetal position. She shivered under the pink quilt he'd bought this afternoon at Riley's Boutique in town.

"I'm here," he said softly.

"He's never going to stop searching for me," she mumbled. "Please, help me. Please, don't make me go back. Don't—" She gasped. Her body jerked and then she screamed in agony.

He placed his hand on her shoulder, wishing for her pain and fears to vanish. "I'm right here, protecting you, Aurora."

She seemed to be so deep in a nightmare, not even his presence roused her, which was strange. His presence always brought peace and tranquility to his people. Evil and darkness couldn't survive for long when he was near. He detected no darkness in her spirit, yet she fought some kind of evil hiding deep inside her, or maybe she fought the trauma of losing her parents. But still, she should've calmed with only his touch, yet, she didn't. She continued to shake as incoherent words tumbled from her lips.

He'd never been so moved to comfort a person in his life as he was right then. Instead of letting her work through the fear and pain and cleanse it with her own white light in her own time, he sat on the bed and focused his own energy to quicken her natural cleansing process.

While he sat with his hand on her shoulder, he focused on untying the dark ribbons that had knotted and tightened within her spirit and were cinching around her chest and neck, attempting to snuff the life from her. He wasn't going to lose her. He remained determined to rid the dark energy clinging to her. With his angelic gift as a Law Enforcement Angel, he began to search for the root of the darkness in her dreams. The deeper he searched, the more he uncovered her own special gifts from God. She was born special, like him. Her soul was as pure as an angel.

Oh my…you're an angel, like me. Well, you're at least part angel, if not a full-fledged angel. You feel like you're born of two angels, like me. But you can't be. Your father was as far from an angel as a person could get. Unless your father isn't biologically related to you. If he isn't, then who is your father? What kind of angel are you? What kind of angel was your mother? How did she hide her abilities from me? What were her powers? What are your powers?

"Daddy, please don't…don't tell. Please, don't tell," she begged as she slept.

While he lifted her onto his lap, he curled the pink quilt under her. He held her against his chest, wrapping his arms tightly around her to comfort her. But he wanted more than to just comfort her, he wanted to be closer, skin-to-skin. "I'm here for you. You're safe with me. Nothing can harm you now. I promise that nothing and no one will ever harm you while you're with me."

His mind raced. *What did her father do to her? I hope he didn't use her like he tried to use me. I was so young when I met him. My parents warned me that he couldn't control his impulses.*

"Daddy, no. I don't want to," she mumbled. The torment in her tone wounded his heart.

Logan was sure her father took advantage of Aurora's naïveté and her mother's love. The man probably offered them up for whatever gifts they had as angels, instead of money in a poker game. Her father always managed to do something terrible and then asked for forgiveness in an attempt to stop following the dark path. But he wasn't strong enough to resist the desire to delve back into the underground world filled with the devil's false promises. The man held too much pride to ask for help. And he always refused help when offered. He had to do everything on his own. He never got down on his knees and truly repented to God for his sins. He never prayed for deliverance from the devil. He never asked for my intervention, my...

He shut me out all those years ago. He shut me out as his pregnant wife begged him to listen to me, to protect his family. And now the only one left from his family is this precious woman who might not even know what she is or why she was targeted along with her parents.

She exhaled, blowing warm air against his neck,

pulling him from his thoughts and instantly heating him up in a way that he had to resist. She needed a protector, not a lover.

Aurora Smith, I need to find you a husband. This arrangement is not going to work between us. I don't know what kind of angel blood is inside you, but I need a full-fledged healing angel to marry. And it's highly unlikely you're one of those. I doubt God would hand me one to protect, especially not one who is barely an adult, not one ten years younger than me...would He?

Her trembling stopped, but a full body shudder coursed through him with desire unlike he'd ever experienced. The ribbons of fear clogging up her spirit vanished, replaced with an aura as pure as freshly fallen snow sent from the heavens above on God's command. And that moment changed him. He had to keep her safe, and in order to do that, she needed to remain within his territory and under his protection. She needed to join his church, adding another layer of protection for her. And above all else, he needed to find out what kind of powers she held, and if she knew she was an angel.

Her lips brushed against his neck, and out of nowhere, a fire within him ignited. He pulled her closer, wanting nothing more than to take her to his bed and make her his wife.

I want you, Aurora. I want to make a family with you.

He inhaled, attempting to smother the fire inside him, but it just burned hotter the more he tried to extinguish the flames.

She's just eighteen. This has to be a reaction to meeting someone like me. How are you so pure of spirit? Your mother's spirit absorbed the darkness, and your father had so much darkness. Living with him would taint her and you. Loving him would change her life's essence. It would muddy her spiritual light until she had none left…

"Logan?" Aurora mumbled.

"It's me," he replied. "You were—"

"Please let me stay."

He parted his lips, ready to respond, but she mumbled something he didn't understand before he realized she'd been talking in her sleep. He didn't want to leave her, but he needed some distance. He wanted to claim her and he couldn't do that.

"Logan," she whispered inside a deep moan.

Blood rushed to his cock. *I can't be this close to you. There is something between us that I can't explore.*

Swiftly, he maneuvered her under the covers and tucked her in without her waking.

Gazing at the blonde-haired beauty, he lingered beside the bed wishing he wasn't obligated to be her guardian, her protector, her judge and jury. Soon she would know his role in the community, in his church, and in the country. It would be difficult for her to live under his rules, and she'd have to live by them soon enough. His rules would have to be followed, although it would be her choice whether to follow the rules or be punished by him.

Watching her sleep, he worried that she would refuse to join his church. That he'd probably be giving up his desire for a perfect match for a not-so-okay match because there were no compatible female angels available. He worried that Aurora might end up like him—lonely. He worried that if she stayed in his house, she might be living with a woman he'd have to punish often because she sought out the darkness when life didn't go her way. He secretly hoped that the woman he was friends with would find a perfect match or even a partial match within the church so she wouldn't be an option for him to date or marry. He knew in his heart that marrying that woman would be a terrible mistake. But loneliness weakened even men like him—Law Enforcement Angels.

She shifted and the fabric of her T-shirt pulled tightly against her full breasts. His mouth watered, ready to lick her curves, to suck her tits, to make love to every inch of her body, to create a baby with her. He shook his head, attempting to erase the thoughts of Aurora as *his* to love.

I'm so desperate to find love that I'm looking at this beautiful young woman and lusting after her. Lord, help me.

"I want you to be mine to love forever." He shouldn't have spoken those words. But saying them cooled some of the burning desire inside his soul. He had to speak the truth. It was part of his job, of his nature, of the law he loved and followed. But he couldn't stop thinking about the reality of his bleak future.

Maybe he'd remain single for the rest of his life. Maybe his purpose was to protect Aurora and make sure she only accepted a one hundred percent perfect match for her husband within the church's congregation. She'd remain alone like him until she was old enough to manage her gifts. Maybe they'd find out what her gifts were together. She would learn to be strong while being around people who wanted the evil exorcised from their spirits, but who struggle to stay away from the devil's temptation. Then she'd stay for the same reasons as he did—because he loved the church, this town, and the people. She'd stay because her desire for a family of her own wasn't as important as her duty to protect and care for those doing good in this world.

Aurora stretched her limbs, taking up more space on the bed. A flutter of passionate pink and red ribbons appeared in her aura. A sultry moan fell from her lips, sending his cock pumping more and more blood into its muscle.

He managed to turn around and walk into the bathroom and close the door before he did something rash, like kiss her. The need for her touch, for her moan to be because of him, pushed him into doing something he hadn't...ever. He unzipped his jeans and fisted his cock, gliding up and down and up and down along the shaft.

I want her. God, I want her. I want her to be mine. I won't be satisfied until she is all mine. No one else but a perfect match within the church will do for her and that will never happen. God, please, make her mine. I don't care that she's not perfect for me. I'll take her as she is. Give her either a perfect match or have her choose me.

CHAPTER FOUR

Aurora

After dreaming of Logan Hutchison *all night long,* she'd woken up with a fervent need to wash off the lust and sweat from the things she and he did in her fantasies. She remained so focused on washing away her desire that she didn't pay any attention to the closed door. In fact, she didn't think about her surroundings at all. She just opened the bathroom door like she would've done with her parents and walked to the shower. She lifted the hem of her damp T-shirt, ready to slough off her sweaty clothes, when she stopped, spotting the star of her dreams.

Logan held a toothbrush under the water on his side of the sink, staring at her in the mirror.

Silently apologizing, she gazed back at him, sweeping over his athlete's body. She memorized each gorgeous dip and valley along his chest and abs, daydreaming with more accurate details than in her dreams…clinging to his sides as he pressed his naked body against hers. Only he wasn't fully nude. The man wore jeans that hugged his ass like it was happy to be there. And she couldn't blame the fabric. She'd be happy, too, if she were his jeans.

As soon as she'd spent more than her share of time admiring his backside, her gaze drifted to his chest and lingered once more. But she needed another look downward. And she indulged her desires, unable to stop from following the ridges and valleys of rippling abs she wanted to touch, to the muscles on his sides that she'd clung to as he parted her legs, to his waistband that narrowed, calling to her to unbutton those jeans, to the bulge he unleashed in her dreams and plunged deep inside her. She sucked in her bottom lip and squeezed her thighs together, remembering the intensity of the moment, of the passion. The moan on her tongue was closed off, but she felt it begging to come out.

The worst part was he saw her taking her time, memorizing every inch of skin he had on display. When she realized that he'd turned off the water and stood staring straight at her, the amount of heat that rose to her cheeks had to have made them a cornucopia of deep shades of red.

She cleared her throat. "Sorry, sir." *Not sorry. Looking at you is well worth the embarrassment of being caught.*

"We're going to town in a few minutes," he mumbled. Then he left the bathroom and stepped into his bedroom, closing the bathroom door behind him.

The good news was that he wasn't addicted to her. From that interaction, she concluded that the man couldn't get away fast enough. But to be fair, she interrupted him in his morning routine, and he lived alone. Plus, she didn't follow his rule to knock before opening the door. And it was his house and his rules, which he followed.

Mom was like Logan in that she thrived on routine. And things were good when she had one, but Dad wasn't much for anything repetitive or steady. Aurora loved her dad, but when he was stuck between a rock and a hard place, the man wasn't thinking about saving his family. He only looked for an exit he could get through; everyone else was on their own. It was sad, but his instinctive-priority was always self-preservation. Honestly, the man was a hot mess, and she and her mom spent most of their time trying to clean up all the spiritual dirt he brought home. And sometimes they power cleaned him and got most of the dirt off, allowing him to walk a well-lit path...for a while. Unfortunately, those easier times were so few that she had a hard time remembering them.

But today was a new day, and Logan didn't seem to be anything like her father, which was probably why he and Dad hadn't talked much in the last several years. The past didn't matter today because gorgeous Logan Hutchison was taking her on a trip to town, and she hoped to learn as much about the man and the people in the community as she possibly could. The more she knew, the more she'd be able to gauge the threat each person posed. And if the heat inside her body meant anything, she hoped to find out if it was just him that made her feel things in her girlie parts that she'd never felt before, or if she was going through some kind of delayed sexual puberty. Or maybe it was a byproduct of a stage of grief from the trauma she'd recently experienced—although she'd never heard of anything like that happening.

She hopped in the shower and turned the temperature to cold. Washing up in the frigid temperatures reduced the heat burning through her system, which pleaded with her to make some kind of excuse to undress in front of Logan in hopes he'd want her as a girlfriend or wife. But the heat still burned inside her as she dried off and dressed. Something deep within her had changed. Maybe it was turning eighteen. Or maybe the desire for the man was because she knew in her heart that he could and would protect her, because the evil man was coming. She might not know when, but he would come, or she would have to go to court to see him. He would demand her attendance. And she wasn't strong enough to fight him alone.

CHAPTER FIVE

Aurora

From its inception, the city of Exorcise, Texas was set on a square grid with the classical white church with a steeple and cross, where Logan worshiped, standing as the center point.

According to Logan, the founders bought the land after receiving a vision from God that this would be a place of redemption and safety. More visions had come to the founders, and with each vision, buildings were erected, people came, and stayed. But one thing Logan had emphasized while he told Aurora of the history of the city, was that each person who called Exorcise home or who visited, either chose to follow the rules of the church or they didn't cross the county line. If a person had decided to go against the rules of the land and crossed into Exorcise, Texas, God marked the person's aura, alerting Logan to escort the person outside the county limits and contact the police in the neighboring communities that there might be trouble. If that marked person committed a crime within Exorcise, then Logan arrested, judged, and handed out the sentence, immediately. If for any reason Logan wasn't available, his grandfather stepped in and stood in Logan's place.

When she asked how one person could do all that when in the United States there was a judicial system in place and a process that must be adhered to, he stated that the United States recognized Exorcise, Texas as its own entity, a holy entity like Vatican City. No rules of any country or other religion in the world existed in Exorcise. God had set the city apart as His, along with its inhabitants. The rules of the church were God's rules and they were obeyed or the Enforcer of the Law otherwise known as the Sheriff, who was Logan, carried out the punishment.

To be a hundred percent honest, the man's words scared her. She hadn't thought about the town's laws when she drove here. She didn't know any of their rules, or if maybe she'd broken one since she arrived. But then again, Logan told her that most crimes committed in town were minor and caused by teens who were testing their boundaries, or by an adult who was struggling with an issue—both instances where the judgment cast down was a conversation with him and the two parties in question.

The town was safe, and there'd only been one instance of real evil touching their community, but that in the end good won over that particular evil. A new level of cosmic protection arrived as soon as the threat had been eliminated, and that the next day is when the markings began.

She wasn't sure whether she should be suspicious or treat him like he was crazy, because what he had told her would sound insane to most people. But she wasn't most people, and he might know it.

In fact, she couldn't remember what she'd told him about the man who planned to find and take her. The same man who murdered her parents. She was such a mess when she spoke to Logan that she could've spilled the tea about her whole weird life. She could've told him that she believed the man to be a demon. So, instead of pretending she didn't accept God's role in the history of this place, she nodded, trusting that he told the truth. And she believed that God's presence came over this land when faced with danger, *and* that he appointed Logan in charge to judge people fairly.

The moment she accepted his version of the history of Exorcise, Texas, something seemed to change in Logan. The bright white aura surrounding him that expanded wherever they went, remained the same, but he walked closer to her and placed his hand on her back, leading her where he wanted her to go.

In the center stood an impressive, white church with a beautiful flower garden for the public to enjoy in the front. To the right and left of the blooming garden were boutiques, a hardware shop, a grocery store, and the one hotel in town. As her tour guide, Logan pointed out the small businesses, which was every business allowed within a hundred-mile radius of the church. There were no chain stores allowed in the small town. Everyone had a job to do and they did it.

He led her into one boutique after another to gather the items she needed for everyday life on his ranch.

Shopping for necessities proved to have multiple embarrassing moments for her in front of Logan. Everyone she encountered knew Logan on a first-name basis. He introduced her as his guest, residing in his home, which garnered curious smiles from the saleswomen, and winks from the older salesmen. But the admission of her status as *his guest* stressed her out because she wanted to stay permanently, and being a guest suggested her time under his protection was temporary.

The worry was short lived because soon permanent embarrassment would call victory during the shopping adventure, wishing Logan was as far away as possible from her. He led her into the lingerie store where all things sexy and beautiful lived. A pretty redhead took Aurora's hand, leaving Logan at the front of the store. Luckily, Aurora was the only customer.

"Make sure she has everything she needs for church and the ranch and whatever else she might need," Logan said.

The heat in Aurora's cheeks burned brightly.

"No worries, Logan. She's in good hands," the redhead said. She looked at Aurora, seemingly assessing her needs. She plucked a crimson silk bra and panties that looked far too expensive for Aurora and guided her past an older lady gathering panties and bras and nighties to a fitting room in the back of the store.

"Are you staying in here with me?" Aurora asked.

"Do you know your bra size?" the redhead asked.

"No, ma'am. My mom always bought my clothes."

"Take off your shirt and leave your bra on," She pulled the measuring tape from around her neck.

So far, the woman didn't give off any vibes of addiction, but Aurora hesitated. "I've never done this before. What are you going to do?"

"I'm going to measure you for a perfect fit."

With a big inhale and prayer that Logan would protect her, Aurora raised her shirt over her head and placed the shirt on the upholstered chair in the corner near the mirror.

"That bra is too small for you." The redhead wrapped the tape around her chest in different places. Then she wrapped it around Aurora's waist and hips. "We're going to trash those panties and bra. You're not walking out in them. So, what is your favorite color?"

"White. But that's not really a color. It's a shade, so pink and gold and silver are my favorites. I also love green like the Georgia grass in springtime. I like lavender and lemon and violet."

She laughed. "You need to go to the nursery and pick out herbs for a garden. Logan will make a place for it on his ranch. All you need to do is ask. Oh, and go to Sarah's boutique. There is a T-shirt with herbs printed on it. I have lingerie that matches it." She parted the red curtain and peeked her head out. "Olga, she's a thirty-two 'D' and a small for panties."

The older lady grabbed a white lace bra and panties set along with a pale-pink silk nightie made for seduction and passed by Logan. "She's beautiful, Logan. And she's sweet."

Logan nodded and Aurora caught his eye. But if she could see him, then he could see her in her bra. She covered her arms over her chest and backed to the side behind the curtain.

Ugh. What a disaster. I'm never going to be able to look him in the eye again.

To his credit, Logan had acted bored during the exchanges. But she could tell that he listened and seemed to notice everything that everyone did around him, including her. The tilt of his head toward a person speaking, a shift of his feet in the direction of a chime noting a door opening or closing, or a quick glance her way revealed his constant watch and awareness of his surroundings.

Aurora tried on the undergarments and walked out wearing a white bra and matching panties beneath her clothes.

The redhead handed Logan a big bag. "Her size is on file, so if she needs anything, just call and we'll make sure we have it. Thanks for coming in."

"Thanks for your help. I'm sure Aurora will be shopping here often." Logan led Aurora out and to the next store. The man bought her everything a woman would need and most of the time, he walked around the store, greeted everyone and then picked up a bag full of supplies or clothes at the register. He bought her clothes she touched but the price stopped her from trying it on.

While she walked by his side, she noticed that the townsfolk liked and respected him. The feeling seemed mutual, as Logan seemed to like and respect everyone in the community—at least from what Aurora could read of their auras during his conversations or polite handshakes and hugs. He paid for her clothes and bathroom supplies without flinching at the prices, but she had sticker shock. The small town had a lot of high-end retail boutiques and none of the inexpensive box stores where she always shopped.

Honestly, she'd never owned anything as nice as what he'd bought her and probably never would again. It would take her years to pay him back for all the stuff in the bags. She'd never fit everything into a backpack.

The realization that he'd insisted on buying her more than she needed almost brought her to tears. Not only did it mean that she would have something to hang up in the closet, but it meant that he expected her to stay with him for more than a couple days or even a month. Sure, remaining in his home for more than a week might be temporary for his standards, but it wasn't temporary for hers.

While he led her back to his truck in the church's parking lot, she spotted the college where she planned to attend in the nearby distance. "Did I tell you that I applied to the college here?"

"Yeah. I checked on your application while you were trying on clothes. They've got everything they need and are looking at how much they're going to offer you in scholarships."

"Scholarships? Am I accepted?" *How could that be possible? I applied late.*

He opened the passenger car door. "Yes. You're accepted. But you didn't declare a major, so they're deciding which major to place you in. You might get a call in the next couple weeks to discuss your academic aspirations."

"Huh...I haven't really thought that far ahead." She climbed into the truck and placed the last of the shopping bags on the floorboard next to her feet.

He closed her door and jogged around the front of the truck, hopped in to his seat, and started the engine. "You can think about it. There's no rush. Is there anything else that you might need in town before we head back to the ranch?"

You bought me everything I asked for and a bunch of stuff I needed but was too embarrassed to mention. Heck, you bought me three months' worth of tampons. Not even my father bought me feminine supplies. Mom always did that and it was only a small box at a time. I had to be able to fit it into my backpack with the necessities. "I can't think of anything."

"I know you weren't brought up in the church, but I'd like for you to come with me on Wednesdays and Sundays. I'd like for you to learn about our laws and what we believe. If you like what you hear, you could join. Although there's no pressure to join—only to go. But it's a great church, and I hope you'll give it a chance."

"Dad wasn't much for church and neither was Mom, but I've always wanted to go. Mom said that she'd take me here, to Exorcise, someday, and she'd drop me off to experience a church service. She said it was the only church she'd encountered where God's presence could be felt."

Dad had said that all churches were under Satan's rule. To never trust anyone who went to church. But privately, when it was just Aurora and her mother, her mom refuted his comments, telling her that God could carry all their burdens, if they just asked. Her mother said that her father never asked God to carry his burdens, and that she stopped asking God to carry hers long ago. Her mother told her that she believed she deserved God's judgment for the choices she made. That she was sorry for all the mistakes she'd made. That God would accept

Aurora into His house here on earth, even if she wasn't around to see it. She seemed to know death would come for her, as if she had a premonition about having a short life.

"I'm a bit biased because this is my church, but I agree with your mom about God's presence being felt in my church and town. I go to the early service on Sundays and the late-evening service on Wednesdays," he said. "I'm going to assume you'll join me, unless you tell me otherwise."

"Okay." *That's easy. I've got nothing else to do, and I'm not staying at the ranch alone. I'm going to be stuck like glue to you every minute of every day for the foreseeable future.*

"And, there are other days we could go, if you want to," he said.

"I will go anywhere you want me to go." *I'm not letting you out of my sight. I like you. I'm attracted to you, and I know it's not a mutual attraction but I can live with that. You will never know how much your energy and spirit make me want you for more than a protector.*

"So if I wanted to go every night of the week, you'd go?" he asked.

"Yes, sir. As long as I'm with you, I'll go three times a day, every day, if that's what you'd like." Looking at him, she couldn't stop thinking he was built like a fortress of steel.

Dad always bragged that you were the strongest man and the best shot in all of Texas, which seemed impressive to me considering the size of Texas. Dad didn't seem to be exaggerating about you, probably a first for him.

Logan patted the seat next to him. "Come here."

She unbuckled her seatbelt and slid across the bench

seat next to him. Heat filled the girlie parts that she was trying to ignore. Her heart raced for his touch.

It's only a crush, not love. He's a man who is taking care of me as a favor. He's being extra nice because of what I've been through. I'm probably overreacting and overthinking my crush is really love because I'm totally dependent on his kindness. And he is kind. He's pure of heart. He's—

He put his arm around her. And oh my, his scent was pure vanilla goodness. She snuggled close to him as he drove slowly down the road toward his house.

"I haven't driven you crazy yet?" he asked.

"Nope," she said. *You're quiet. Your presence is soothing. You tell me exactly what to do and when—leaving me no room to question you. You ask me a question, if you want to know something about me you don't already know. You don't assume. You're as close to perfect as I imagined a man could ever get.*

He took a left onto the gravel road to his house and parked next to her small compact car. "Mind if we get you a new car? The one you have isn't practical for driving on the ranch."

"I don't have money for a new car, so it will have to do for now." She'd have to work for a while before she could afford anything new.

"I'll buy it. We can keep your car, if you want, but trading it in for a truck makes more sense. If you're willing to help me around the ranch, another truck would come in handy."

"Are you sure? I'll help you with anything. You don't have to buy me a truck."

"So what's your favorite car color?" he asked.

"I like white or beige or gunmetal or something that blends into the surroundings when I'm driving. Nothing flashy." *Are you really going to buy me a truck?* "I might need some help getting used to driving a big vehicle."

"You'll do fine." He turned off the engine, but remained sitting and holding her. "We need to talk."

You're ready for me to leave. You don't want me around. I'm your guest, and Dad always said that guests have a three day limit before they start smelling like rancid fish. I don't want to be rancid fish.

CHAPTER SIX

Aurora

"What would you like to talk about?" she asked. *Here's where you talk about my exit plan. Did you already find me a new place to live? I'd rather you become addicted to me. Then maybe you'd try to kidnap me. I'd gladly sleep with you every night of my life.*

"Did your mom or dad tell you about our church, other than God's presence is felt there?" he asked.

Ok. This is good. You're not getting rid of me. You're concerned about my spiritual wellbeing. "A little."

"Did either mention the differences between churches across the globe, and how mine is different? About the open nature of it? About our rules?"

"Neither said much about denominations, differences, or rules. They both talked about leaving the church because it wasn't for them. That's about it. I know basics about different religions and faiths, but I've never stepped foot in a church or any other house of worship as far as I know." *Aren't all churches open? Whenever I walked by one, the doors were always open and people were coming and going seven days a week.*

"We only have one church in town and pretty much everyone eighteen or older in the community is a member. There are certain vows that we are compelled to take when we join the church here. Some of our sister churches don't require their members to uphold the stringent guidelines we have for our congregation. But God set this one aside, as *His*." He opened the car door and stepped out. He held out his hand to her as though he were about to anchor Aurora from floating adrift in the middle of rough waters. The conversation seemed to be getting much more serious than she'd expected.

As she placed her hand in his, a spark of electricity ignited flames at his touch and seemed to strengthen her connection, binding their hands together as one. Instead of releasing his hand, she squeezed it tighter, not wanting to lose the connection.

While he helped her out of his side of the truck, he slid his other arm around her, supporting her back and pulling her closer to him.

Gazing up at his serious face, she wanted to curl her arms around his neck and go in for a kiss, but she didn't. She waited.

He seemed to hesitate to let her go, but he eventually released her, severing the connection and placing distance between them. He stepped backward and shifted to the side, guiding her body easily into a position to follow him. He seemed to silently tell her he wasn't interested in her as anything other than his houseguest. So, she reluctantly accepted her place in his life as he led her to the porch.

"Take off your boots before you come into the house and place them next to mine," he ordered. "You'll be wearing these for chores on the ranch."

Following his lead, she placed the new boots he'd bought her and insisted she wear today next to his on the mat beside the door.

He opened the door and guided her into the gigantic living room with a sparse amount of furniture. Once inside, the room didn't seem so small with him in it. His presence filled up the empty space.

"You haven't asked me any questions about the church," he said.

"I didn't know I was supposed to. I figured you'd tell me what I needed to know."

He sat on the gray modern-style couch in the dove-white painted room. The room didn't really feel like he decorated it, but it was simple and pretty.

Did a girlfriend decorate the room? I don't see you choosing a gray color for your living space. You seem to like white and a blueish white or maybe a little pink like me. I bet you like all the soft, happy shades of white, like me. Although I do like a lush green, but only for clothes and plants, not furniture. Do you like plants? Herbs? Spices?

She sat on the only other furniture in the room—the matching gray ottoman in front of him.

"What are your stringent guidelines?" She planned to join the church, no matter how strict or silly the rules. She hoped to be his shadow, going everywhere he went. Maybe she'd find a job at the church and ask to work whenever he was there. That'd be a win-win in her book.

"Every woman who is single and of marriage-age wears thin white clothes with no undergarments during services. When a member turns eighteen, they're given physical and psychological tests to find their perfect match within the church's complex matchmaking system. Every year after that initial testing, if the member hasn't married, they retake the tests and go on dates with the other single men or women available in the church who are either semi-matches or have a mutual attraction. Some find matches to members in sister churches through the database or bring in a person from somewhere else to join *my* church."

"That's why you bought me a bunch of white dresses?"

"Yes. And if you join, you could be matched with a man who is eighteen or a man who is fifty or even sixty," he said. "Are you still willing to go to church with me? To potentially join?"

"I could refuse to date or marry someone picked for me, right?" she asked. *I doubt I'll get picked for marriage.*

"You could make a note to explain your preferences on the testing sheets. I have noted in the comment section of the psychological testing that I will only allow a blindfold and automatic church-sanctioned marriage ceremony for a one hundred percent perfect match within the Exorcise Church database. I can choose to either marry someone partially matched or even not at all matched. But only if I were to find someone I'd felt would be a good companion who would be willing to sacrifice a perfect match for an okay-one. Perfect matches are rare, very rare."

"What if my perfect match is ugly, and I'm not the slightest bit attracted to him? If he is, I'm not going out with him or marrying him. They'll have to deal with you, too. I'm not going on a date alone."

"I'm not going to be joining you on your dates, whether you're matched with more than one man or not." He shook his head in what seemed like confusion as he half-laughed.

"Yes, you are," she said. "I'm not meeting anyone without you."

The smile that spread across his lips made her think he might be pleased by the conversation. But upon further analysis, his pleasure could have easily been a figment of her imagination. She wanted him to like that she needed and wanted his opinion and approval.

"Are you a virgin?" he asked. "That is one of the questions on the evaluation that you'll have to fill out to become a member."

"Yes, I am, and I'm proud of it." She stood up and held her head high. "I have standards when it comes to men. My mother taught me that love isn't something you should ever compromise on. So I'll only accept a perfect match, or I'll never be intimate with a man or get married. I have no idea what I'm going to do from here on out, but I do know I'm remaining a virgin until I'm someone's wife." *I'd consider giving up my virginity to you. But you're my one exception. The only exception. I think I love you.*

"What if your husband hasn't made that same commitment? What if he's had sex with a lot of women prior to meeting you?" He raised his right brow and held that tight, semi-amused smile. But he leaned toward her as if he couldn't wait to hear her answer.

"I don't care. I'd actually prefer if he knew what he was

doing. I'd want to be taught and guided through my first time with someone who knows all about it."

"What if he's a virgin?" He brushed his hand over his mouth and chin, dropping his gaze for an instant.

Her cheeks burned so hot, they had to be on fire, but she wasn't about to be the first to back down from embarrassment in this conversation. She'd hold to her personal truths and standards, no matter what anyone thought about them being nearly impossible to match.

Are you a virgin? Are you waiting for marriage? Are your standards as high as mine?

"Then we'll learn about sex together," she said. "It might not be what I prefer, but I'm good either way."

"Hmm... You're good either way? Are you truly comfortable being matched with a virgin?"

Instead of looking closer at her like her father would have when he didn't believe her, Logan leaned back and seemed to widen his view of her. Something about what she said must have made him back away. She couldn't tell if he thought she was a liar, or if he wanted to verify her answer because it surprised him.

The colors of his aura shifted from the usual stark and brilliant white to an equally bright and beautiful gold, then smatterings of pink and red hues appeared and disappeared within seconds of each other. She had no idea what to think of those colors and wondered if he had the ability to hide, manipulate, or close off portions of his aura from others—from people like her.

"I really am okay with marrying either a virgin or a not-a-virgin. I doubt I'd match with anyone. I'm focused on my lack of a career path at the moment. That and staying alive."

"Don't worry about your safety. No one will ever get past me." The man's aura didn't change as he spoke. The confidence he exuded remained, as if her worries about being found or kidnapped were no longer an issue.

He raised his brows and scrubbed his hand over his mouth and down his throat and chest. He seemed to fidget a little. Pink and red ribbons of light floated around the bright golden expanse of his aura and then all the color morphed into the normal white light, leaving him coated in the brilliant purity of goodness that seemed to live within him. She'd even wager a guess that his blood wasn't crimson, but was white and pure as the heavens.

"If you're interested, the church can counsel you on a career," he said. "Through the testing, you'll learn what careers would best suit you. Some people consider our church a cult, but it's not. You can join or not join, visit or leave, at your discretion. You'll always be welcomed by everyone, regardless of whether you're a member or not."

"Why are you single?" She sat back down on the gray ottoman. *You're handsome and strong, and smart and sexy.*

"There are several reasons, but the main one is that I haven't found a perfect match. I won't move from Exorcise, Texas or this church, so I've been waiting for my special someone to become a member or turn eighteen and get the testing, proving we're perfect matches. I've considered finding someone who isn't a perfect match and marrying, but something has always prevented me from following through..." He seemed to want to elaborate, but he held his tongue.

"Have you had sex?"

"Yes, Aurora, I have." He frowned, but the energy around him never changed. He wasn't angry she'd asked, but he didn't seem pleased about it either. "There's a service tonight. I'd like you to come with me."

"Okay," she said. "If I want to join after the service, may I?"

"Yes. But if you do, you'll have to stay and go through the testing. It could take several hours. You'll be examined for verification of your virginity and be put into the database for marriage. You're eighteen, and it doesn't matter what you've been through or are comfortable doing. If you have a perfect match, you'll be married as soon as both you and your match are present inside the church. It's a big decision. Perfect matches are extremely rare, but they do happen. It's a life-long commitment to not only God, but also the church, and your spouse. And the ceremony in our church is one of faith. You'll be blindfolded without ever seeing your perfect match. You won't know what he looks like before you've committed your life to him. You'll make love to him during a silent ceremony while wearing the blindfold. Do you have that kind of faith?"

If you have faith in the process and in God, then I do, too. I'm doing whatever you tell me to do. I'm joining the church tonight, adding in the caveat of a marriage only if I have a one hundred percent perfect match. When no one is my match, then I'll come back and live with you forever. But I better ask more questions, or you'll think I'm even weirder than I am.

"What if I'm matched with more than one person?" she asked.

"You'll have the choice of dating both men to see if you prefer one over the other for marriage. You might end up in a triad marriage with two men, or a man and another woman, or two other women."

"Oh." *I don't know that I want that.*

"Those matches are even more rare, and your testing has to show that you're open to those types of relationships." He leaned forward, his face so close to hers that she could feel the warmth of his breath. "I've got to feed and put the animals up for the night. I'd like you to put on one of the white dresses with nothing underneath."

Her heart nearly stopped. Her breath definitely quit on her. Dang. She shuddered with an image of him undressing her, with him carrying her to his bed and ravishing her.

He stood up and her lips were so close to the big bulge between his legs that if she weren't frozen from his earlier words, she could have licked it. And to her surprise, she wanted to lick him, even over the denim.

She swallowed and raised her chin, catching her breath and gazing up at his stoic face. "What if I have a perfect match in the church?"

"Then you'll be going home married to him. It's a big commitment to accept membership. Your father declined membership his entire life." He looked away. "He married outside the church." He shrugged and met her gaze once more. "But your mother was special, and you brought more love and happiness to them than they ever thought possible. Your parents loved you very much."

Her dad loved her mom. He loved her, too, but not nearly as much. He had too much darkness that followed him around everywhere to be able to focus on his family. He had internal demons he couldn't shake no matter how hard he tried. Greed haunted him. Love was an afterthought.

"Are the regular close-to-perfect type matches rare?" she asked.

"They aren't *rare* at your age, but they aren't common either. Matches happen more often in my age group. Your parents were young when they had you. I'm six years younger than your father. I skipped a couple grades in elementary school and then in high school, too." He glanced at the door and back at her. "I've got to go or we'll be late for the service."

"Okay. I can wear makeup, right?" She rose from the ottoman and walked toward her bedroom.

"Yes, ma'am. Just wear a white dress with nothing underneath."

"White boots?" she asked.

"Or white sandals," he said. "Wear your hair down."

She pivoted, getting a quick glance at his backside as he stepped outside and closed the door.

I'd marry you in a second. You're the hottest man I've ever seen.

She walked to her bedroom and flopped on her bed. "I want to be your perfect match, Logan Hutchison." She sighed. But she promised her mom that she'd never marry a human, like her mom did. Logan was human—a perfect human—but a human all the same.

I'm going to talk to the minister in charge and secretly request a date with Logan. Maybe that's too bold for the first testing. Next year, I'll ask. That's too long to wait. Maybe I'll ask in a couple months. I'll have to see how people date within the church and then make a decision whether to speak to a minister about my feelings for Logan. Maybe I could marry a human. Just because it didn't work out with Dad, doesn't mean it wouldn't work out with Logan.

CHAPTER SEVEN

Aurora

hile she sat behind an antique wooden desk with her newly pierced nipples poking through slits the piercer cut in her white dress so that the golden cross nipple rings hung on display, she waited for the men considered perfectly suited to be her husband to enter the room with the priest. Either the men would choose which would marry her, or she would decide which one she preferred to spend the rest of her life loving. From the results of the testing, none of them were open to a triad marriage.

The virginity verification and bloodwork had been done after the written testing. The priest seemed excited about her initial test results and told her there were matches within the congregation.

The door opened and the priest walked in alone and closed the door.

What is going on? Where are my matches? She rose from her seat, covering her breasts with her hands. "Is everything okay?"

The redheaded priest smiled, and, out of nowhere, peace settled inside her. "It's better than okay. You have two perfect matches within the congregation. One, we ruled out because of the significant age difference. He isn't interested in marrying an eighteen-year-old, nor should he be. He's much older than you, and he's a widower who is still grieving. So, you truly have one perfect match. He's twenty-eight and never been married. He desires children. He holds an important role in our local and national church. The adjustment might be rocky at first, but he's a good man and will be kind to you."

Ten years older isn't bad. I hope he's good looking. I have to trust the process. I put it on my testing papers. "When do I get to meet him?"

"Right now." He walked toward her and held out his hand. "Come. You'll be blindfolded and undressed, just as he will be."

"I don't get to meet him first? See him?" *I actually got two perfect matches? How is that possible? I marked the box that asked if I was an angel, not the one with the human box. Logan said that perfect matches were extremely rare. Wouldn't angel matches be even more rare? Will Logan be at the ceremony? Did I get matched with an angel or human? But I told them I didn't want to be matched with a human. I even wrote it in my essay about what I was looking for in a perfect match. How is this possible?*

The priest stopped before her. "No, you don't get to meet or see him, prior to the ceremony. You signed the documents, as did he. You're already legally married. As soon as you two make love in front of the elders and have wedding bands placed on your ring fingers, you'll be blessed by God and married. You'll make love again, and afterward, your blindfolds will be taken off, revealing your spouse. It's a test of your faith in God's choice for your partner. Your spouse's faith has been tested over and over in his lifetime. He is ready. There will be no speaking until the blindfolds are removed. Are you prepared to make this lifetime commitment?"

"Does he know anything about me?" she asked. "Does he know that I'm part-angel?"

"He does *not* know who he was perfectly matched to, or that you are an angel, only that he is perfectly matched to a member of our congregation. Also, he is aware that six females out of the twelve who started the testing have completed the process and that only one had a perfect match and that match was with him."

Having completed the intense testing, she could see how a person would quit before finishing the entire process. If she hadn't been so motivated to join the church after the service, she might have quit, too. When she found out she was to be pierced to show her new ranking within the church, she cried. She hated needles, pain, and blood, almost equally. But because she made a commitment to the church to faithfully accept God's call to marriage, she managed to make it through the piercing without calling for Logan to take her home.

So much of the process revolved around blind faith in God's choices for her future. She'd had so many questions about the testing and questions posed on the exams, half of the responses the priest gave her were for her to listen to God's voice telling her which answer to choose. She realized why her mom and dad didn't want to become members—neither would've finished the written exam, let alone the lab tests, virginity verification, or the isolation in a private room for hours awaiting the test results. The process was a lot for her, and she liked tests, commitments, rules, and alone time.

"Are you sure there wasn't a mistake with the results? I'm only eighteen." She placed her hand in his. "I thought the perfect matches were rare for my age group."

The priest sighed. "Do you have faith in the process or did you lie?"

"I didn't lie. I have total faith in the process." She'd see Logan at church, and if she needed him to save her from a horrible marriage, he would. He promised he'd protect her, and she believed in and trusted him as much as she now believed in and trusted God. "Is my husband handsome?"

The priest rolled his eyes, but curled his smooth, long fingers around hers. "Handsomeness is subjective. But yes, most people would consider him handsome."

"Thank you."

He cocked his head toward me. "Shall I continue?"

"Yes, please. Sorry for the questions." She cowered a little. *I need to keep my mouth shut from here forth. No one would measure up to Logan, and that's okay. I will love whomever I marry.*

"Silence is a requirement for the ceremony. You can moan and sigh and grunt, but not speak any recognizable words." He led her out of the room and stopped in the hallway. "Undress in silence."

The sudden change of circumstances should have made her uneasy, even scared, but something about the idea that God had given her a perfect match gave her a sense of peace. That and the entire church was filled with auras of pure white light. No one in the place held any darkness. She'd never been in a place like this before. She loved the church and the congregation, even those who weren't members.

She unzipped the back of the dress and carefully slid her nipples and nipple rings from the slits in the fabric, and let it fall to the floor. She couldn't explain the instant healing of the piercings to the piercer, except to say that she had an exceptional immune system which made her heal quickly. She even told the woman about having one incident in school where she was pushed off the top of a slide and fell. The teacher thought her leg was broken, but when she moved, her leg righted itself. The teacher had looked at her strangely that day. Aurora hadn't thought anything of it, but her mom removed her from the school the next day and enrolled in another. It wasn't until she'd seen someone else take a similar fall and their bones didn't heal immediately that she figured out that she was different. Her mother always said that it was because of her powerful immune system that she healed so quickly. But it wasn't the truth, and Mom knew it. The truth was that Aurora was part-angel, as far as she knew, and God had given her many gifts and healing was one of them.

"You're sloughing off the old and stepping forward into the new." The priest reached into the pockets of his purple robe and held up a blindfold. "Place this over your eyes."

She took the blindfold and placed the elastic around

her head. A small adjustment with the strap in her hair and she slid the silky fabric over her eyes, plunging her in darkness. The lack of sight sent her heartbeat skyrocketing.

"You're safe here," the priest whispered. "Everyone in our church would lay down their life to save yours. So have faith, our precious angel Aurora. God has made His decision. All you have to do is to walk His path in faith."

The words he said sounded so simple to follow, but her father and mother struggled to follow God's path. They didn't have faith, not like the people here, not like her.

She nodded. Faith seemed to be the one thing she had in her life. She had faith when she walked to school every day. She had faith with each frequent move to a new apartment, neighborhood, or school. She had faith when she spoke with the police, or when she faced the... *Don't think about the bad. Bad days are behind me. Logan will protect me.* "Logan is in the building, right?"

"Yes. He's in the building. Now, take a deep breath. I'm placing pins in your hair to secure the blindfold. No matter what happens, keep your eyes closed. Do not open them until you're told to."

She reminded herself that she touched the priest and he had no reaction to her. None at all. Besides that, God wouldn't have brought her here only to torture her. If she were in danger, then she'd see a sign of evil within the place. And there was no evil, not even the slightest speck of gray.

"Okay. I'll keep my eyes closed." *I have faith. This is where I'm supposed to be. God will protect me. He sent me to Logan, and Logan promised to protect me, too.*

She nodded as he gently tucked her hair behind her ears and slid the hairpins against her scalp and through her blonde hair, securing the blindfold from moving. If she had known she'd be married today, she would've braided her hair or done something special to it, but she didn't. She let it loose, dangling down to her low back in natural waves, just as Logan had told her to.

He pressed a fatherly kiss to her forehead. "May you be blessed with a lifetime of love and many children." He took her hand. Not even a slight tingle of sensation accompanied the touch, giving her more confidence that this was the right decision. He guided her forward and then to the right, then left, and right. She would be meeting her husband in minutes. He would be a good man. Logan would make sure of that.

CHAPTER EIGHT

Aurora

The twists and turns, this way and that, along the path leading to the marriage ceremony caused Aurora to lose track of the room from which she'd left. She wouldn't be able to make it out of the building now without someone else showing her the way. Not that she wanted to leave. She didn't. Well, part of her did, but then she thought about all the handsome guys wearing white with their pure bright white auras with colorful ribbons of pink, red, gold, and blue whom she'd seen attending the service. One of those guys might be waiting for her. And although she wasn't great at reading an honest man's interest in her, she thought a couple of them might've been interested in dating her. Maybe one of them was an angel waiting to marry her in the ceremonial wedding chamber. Of course, those guys didn't hold a candle to Logan, but to be honest, no one could compare to Logan Hutchison. Logan was perfect with all his gorgeous muscles and white light that bathed her in safety.

"Lift your foot, but remain quiet," the priest said.

Following his instructions, she lifted her foot and stepped forward, landing on a soft cushion. She continued forward, with both feet on the cushion that she recognized as a soft blanket covering a mattress. This was the place where the ceremony would happen. She'd already signed all the documents and in doing so was already married to the man she was about to meet. But she could still back out. Until they made love, they offered each of them an exit strategy.

The priest placed her hand in a much larger one with rough, calloused fingers.

A familiar spark of electricity heated her body with the touch of her perfect match. Then a sudden shot of adrenaline raced through her veins. One fear vanished from her system—she was definitely attracted to her husband.

A hard body pressed against hers, igniting the fire in her belly. A big, thick rod of muscle poked at her belly, making her imagine that thing moving inside her. Juices flowed between her legs, readying her for the next phase of the ceremony.

A deep exhale blew warm air over her shoulder as he guided her down onto the soft cushion. As soon as her back landed on the soft padding, she heard him moan.

He hovered over her. The heat of his body radiated off him. He shifted, crawling down between her legs. He inhaled and kissed her lower belly. The spark of electricity that struck her hand now struck her belly with his kiss.

More juices flooded her pussy.

She held her tongue, even as she desired nothing else but to whimper and moan. His lips were so soft and gentle as he kissed down her abs toward her—

She stiffened for an instant, as the sensations of his electric kisses on her girlie parts sent a shockwave through her. This was real. He was going to take her. He was going to touch her...*there.*

His kiss on her slit reminded her that this was the last chance to change her path. If she wanted to stop the ceremony, she had to do it now.

Instead of fighting him and refusing the match, she trusted God and Logan and the church that the man on the cushion with her believed with all his heart that she was his perfect partner for life. She inched her legs farther apart, giving him access to the place she'd kept untouched.

As his tongue parted her folds, he moaned. The rich tone of his voice sent vibrations of desire through her, overwhelming her senses. This man knew exactly what to do and where to go next. He had experience in sex—a lot of experience. He was too knowledgeable about her body to be a virgin.

He dipped the tip of his tongue into her sex.

She gasped as new sensations rose within her. With each lick over her clitoris, and every new dive of his tongue into her center, she slowly came undone. The walls of her pussy contracted. Pleasure assaulted her. Juices gushed onto his tongue.

While she arched her back, she spread her legs as wide as she could, readying for more of the newfound love of his mouth between her legs. She liked his mouth. No, she *loved* his mouth. She wanted more of this kind of attention. But instead of continuing to show her his incredible oral skills, he stopped.

She held her breath, hoping he would get back between her legs and make her orgasm again.

In seconds, kisses and licks traveled upward over her belly and breasts. He flattened his tongue, gliding over her nipples, making the crosses on the gold rings jingle. He shuddered over her and dove forward, driving his big cock into her juicy virgin sex.

She squeaked as his cock stretched her so wide, she thought he might have stretched her too far. Another rush of heat and juices flooded her pussy. Then he thrust the huge rod deeper inside her. A strike of pain hit her, as the tip of his cock met the end of her channel.

He rocked back and thrust forward, again and again, grunting louder and louder and louder.

While he seemed to be tearing her slowly in two, she held her breath knowing that the pain would stop at some point. That the information she'd read about sex was indeed the truth.

Unyielding, he thrust into her, grunted, and shuddered. Again and again, he thrust and thrust and thrust in deep rapid succession. A wild roar released from him and then she felt a flooding of hot liquid into her pussy. His cock softened, but only slightly.

Someone grabbed her left hand and slid a ring onto it.

The man making love to her softened his touch, caressing her sides and along her arms until he twined his fingers with hers and squeezed. The man's cock hardened inside her. He rocked back and forth until he thrust deeper and deeper to the end of her channel.

She didn't know what to do and he wasn't showing her. She needed guidance. She expected some sort of supervision. But maybe she was doing everything right? There was a chance that he didn't understand that this was her first time. She squeezed his hand, unsure what else to do.

He released her hands and gripped her hips.

She liked the sudden change. He was going to show her what he wanted her to do with her hips.

Ready to explore a little more of his body, she caressed along the thick muscles of his lower back to his shoulders.

He rolled his hips and thrust.

Following his lead, she pushed her hips down into his thrusts, giving her a new sensation of pleasure. She hooked her leg over his hip and suddenly the head of his cock that remained inside her tunneled in deep. The surface of his shaft touched places that she wanted touched again and again. Pleasure flowed through her, and juices steadily lubricated her channel and entrance. This was what she was waiting for...real pleasure. And she wanted more. Fast and hard and deep.

With a powerful thrust of his cock, he made her moan.

The silence she'd kept the entire time flew out the window. That moan unleashed a rush of fire inside her to let go, to trust him with her body and her heart. She couldn't help from voicing her pleasure in desperate moans.

He exhaled loudly and thrust again and again.

Right there. Oh, yes. Right there. She made a noise that he seemed to like because he thrust faster and faster, driving in deeper and with more passion.

The sultry whimpers and moans she couldn't contain

happened again and again as he seemed to continually target the spot making her repeat that sound.

Unable to stop the sudden blast of bliss rolling like a freight train down the tracks, she writhed, humping and grinding against him, while he thrust. And then a shockwave of power burst from inside her bringing within it a bliss that connected her spirit to his. They were one interconnected being, rolling and rocking, in a mess of moans and grunts.

Her blindfold was removed while they gently rocked through the last moments of pleasure.

"We now pronounce you husband and wife," the priest said. "You may open your eyes."

She opened her eyes. *Prayers do come true.*

"Aurora?" Logan's face drained of color.

Or maybe they don't.

CHAPTER NINE

Aurora

She gazed at the man who'd just made love to her like a beast and now looked like he could vomit because of what they did. Her heart stopped for a moment.

"Yes, Logan. It's me."

Logan Hutchison was her perfect match. Her day couldn't have gotten any better. She already trusted him. She definitely was attracted to him. But it was still a surprise—a happy one for her.

But the shock on his face seemed to rock him to his very core, and not necessarily in a good way. The man looked sick and disappointed and guilty.

I wish you were as happy about this as I am.

He turned his head toward the priest. "Aurora is my perfect match?"

"Yes. One hundred percent," the priest said.

"But I'm—"

"You're perfectly matched as husband and wife," the priest insisted. He stepped to the side and twelve men wearing black robes and white stoles with purple embroidery on them stepped forward.

The priest's words seem to stop Logan from saying more.

Logan's scrutinizing gaze began at her face and then slowly descended her body as he pushed up and sat back on his heels. His hard cock slipped from between her legs and bobbed up against his beautifully formed abs. He closed his eyes and inhaled, seemingly praying in silence.

There was nothing for her to say, so she pushed back away from him and sat up. Blood stained the white velvet blankets over a floor mattress.

Logan opened his blue eyes. "This was unexpected." He stood.

Aurora followed Logan's lead and joined him at his side, a gap of space between them.

Logan shook the priest's hand. "Thank you."

"My pleasure," the priest said. "It was a beautiful ceremony."

While Logan shook all the men's hands, Aurora stood nearby in silence. He led her out of the room and through the church. They were closely followed by the priest and members who observed the ceremony.

"What happened to the other women who were tested?" Logan asked.

"Six decided that they weren't ready for membership at this time," the redheaded priest who managed Aurora's testing said, while they continued moving through the church's inner chambers. "Two matched in the seventy percent range with men in sister churches and are leaving in the morning to marry them. The others had results that showed promise, but they would struggle to make it outside our strict laws. We encouraged our members to reach out to their matches and see if the match would be interested in moving here."

"Oh," Logan mumbled.

"Aurora matched with two from our church. But you and she matched one hundred percent in every category, even age range, which is extremely rare. You even matched within every possible variant within the subcategories, which is, again, extremely rare."

Logan nodded. "I hadn't expected this to be a possibility. I'm Aurora's guardian."

"We're well aware of your surprise at the results and of *Aurora's* as well. Neither of you expected this outcome," the priest said. "Exit through the door as you are and go home. It's been a late night, and as you are well aware, the two of you have to get up early to make the changes in your house that are necessary to keep to our laws." The priest opened the door.

Logan's truck idled by the curb outside.

"Congratulations," the priest said. "We are honored to have witnessed a sacred marriage ceremony within God's house. You and Aurora are indeed blessed by God."

Logan nodded and took Aurora's hand, helping her into the cab of his truck. A spark of electricity skittered through her at his touch, but the jolt of the initial touch dulled quickly as he let go, and she watched him climb into the driver's seat.

Her heart sank into her belly. The man she just

married didn't even look at her as he climbed into the truck. His enthusiasm while they were making love blindfolded had been for one of the other women he knew was being tested. He probably was in a rush to get to church, not for her to experience a service, but to see a woman who planned to join the church today, a woman to be his match.

You love someone else, but you're stuck with eighteen-year-old me.

Logan drove along the outside of the church's perimeter and turned down the main road, taking the long winding road that would eventually lead to his house. They were out long past the community curfew, but she'd learned that the law allowed for exceptions for church members dealing with special circumstances such as weddings with perfect matches.

He parted his lips and then shut them. He opened them again and hesitated but powered onward. "I'm sorry that I have to tell you this now, but you need to know something."

"Okay. What do I need to know?"

"I've been semi-dating someone. I don't really think of it as dating, but we're close. I'd call her more of a friend. A good friend." He sighed. "I need to tell her that I'm married before she hears about it from someone else."

"Sorry." *That girl is getting her heart broken tonight.*

"I'm sorry. I'm stunned that...I hadn't anticipated a perfect match." He glanced at her. "You're gorgeous and young, and I—" He didn't finish his sentence, instead he shifted his focus back on the road. "We'll figure this out."

Looks like I got what I wanted, and you got the short end of the stick.

CHAPTER TEN

Logan

$\mathcal{H}$e should have known the girl he stuffed with his cock wasn't Riley. The electrical short circuit he'd experienced when he touched her hand should've alerted him that it was Aurora. He should've made the connection then because Aurora was the only person he'd ever touched that did that to him. He'd never gone down on Riley, but even then, he should've known it was Aurora because he pretended it was her when he licked her sweet pussy. He didn't want to stop but he also had the uncontrollable desire to be inside her. Right then. He'd never been that way with Riley. Not even once.

In his heart, he knew the perfect match was with Aurora, not Riley. Riley would never be a perfect match with him. She was so far from his kind of perfect. At best, Riley would be a not-so-okay, or not-a-match-but-could-potentially-live-within-his-rules, a sort-of-acceptable-to-date within the church guidelines.

And Riley would have spread her legs instantly for his cock. She would have pulled him into her, not waited to be shown what to do. Riley wouldn't have been so tight, so stiff, so nervous, exactly what he'd wished for in a first time with his wife.

Riley would have fought for dominance, not accepted his. Riley would never be Aurora. But that meant that Aurora was a full-fledge angel. And that would mean that Aurora's mother had been unfaithful, and her mother never struck him as the unfaithful sort.

He parked by Aurora's car and stepped out onto the gravel drive. "Come here." He motioned to her and she scooted over the seat, ready to step down. "I've got you." *I've screwed up enough tonight. I'm going to make it right, starting now.*

He scooped her up into his arms and carried her up the few steps and onto the porch. "This is your home—our home—now and forever."

She kept her gaze down, but her cheeks flushed a pretty pink, the same colors zipping through her aura at lightning speed.

Carrying Aurora over the threshold of his home shouldn't have felt so right, but it did. Everything about the girl made sense, except the fact that she was his estranged friend's daughter—his *dead*, estranged-friend's daughter.

God, please, uncomplicate my emotions when it comes to my wife. Please, make the transition from being single to being married easier for the both of us.

But life was about to get even more complicated for his

marriage. Aurora had a lot to learn and she most likely wouldn't be happy about most of it, when it came to his involvement in the church. And then there's the fact that he's an angel with wings. And she's an angel, too, and he doubted she was aware of that fact.

When Aurora figured out that he's an elder in the church, and that everyone in the local and national church levels, except the priests—and sometimes even them— walk on eggshells around him, she's going to worry and possibly be afraid of him. Enforcing every law in God's name within the church and community came at a cost. As much as people liked him, most were nervous around him.

How can you have been a perfect match with me? You're not rigid or stubborn or—

"Do you need privacy when you call your girlfriend?" she asked.

Woah, Riley wasn't his girlfriend. He'd already forgotten he'd even mentioned Riley to her. But he did need to call her, as a courtesy.

"No. Privacy isn't needed. And she's not my girlfriend, but she and I have been kind of dating on and off over the last several months. Maybe it's been a year?"

"That sounds like a girlfriend to me."

"It's not. She's not and has never been my girlfriend. I've taken her out. We've been intimate. She attends church. Now, she's a member of the church, unless she was one of the women who dropped out. She could've dropped from the testing. She can be stubborn and contrary." He stopped inside his bedroom. It did sound like Riley was his girlfriend, but he never thought of her as one. She was more like a business arrangement. *Ergh...*

He'd been kidding himself thinking he'd ever have even a slight match with Riley, that making her a real girlfriend would be a possibility. There was no way they'd ever be compatible enough for marriage. The church wouldn't have allowed it. If he'd pursued something more with Riley, then he'd have ruined his life and given up on the beautiful woman he now held in his arms. God saved him from his loneliness. He gave him Aurora.

"Do you love her?" She didn't attempt to move from his arms. She waited patiently for his answer, something Riley would never do. Aurora truly was his perfect match, in every way, just like the priest had told him.

"No. I don't love her. We get along. Well, sometimes we like each other. She was one of the other women who went through the testing today. I promised her I'd be at the church service, not that I ever miss church services. I don't. I'm always there. But, she moved here five years ago and has been regularly attending church since she arrived. Last week, she told me that she was joining today, and asked if I would make sure to be there in the unlikely case that we ended up being perfectly matched or at least matched well enough to date with a potential to marry."

"Oh. She was hoping you and she were matched." Aurora bit her bottom lip like he'd seen her do when she was upset, which happened often in the short time since she'd arrived.

Holding back the tears and hurt she felt wouldn't last long, not with all she'd been through recently, and with her propensity to cry out her emotions instead of talk through them. He doubted that he'd have much time to explain his situation with Riley before Aurora released her disappointment and sadness at his confession.

"I knew she wouldn't be a perfect match," he quickly said. "I hadn't expected a perfect match with anyone. I thought I might be put in a pool of men to date her and see what happens. I hadn't expected you to be matched so quickly or..." *I need to shut my mouth. This is not coming out right. I'm into you. I want to do things with you that I've never wanted to do with Riley or anyone else. I'm gonna do things with you...I'm gonna take you to bed and make love to you over and over and over and—*

"Are you disappointed that we're married? You looked like you were going to puke when you saw me."

You don't pull any punches. I feel bad about that. But I do like your honesty.

"I was shocked. I remember when your mom and dad video chatted with me after you were born, and even though I was ten, it still is a vivid memory for me. Your parents were kids when you were born. We all grew up fast..." *I'm making things worse.* "Listen, I know you're vulnerable right now. I claimed your virginity without saying a word."

The memory of that moment was like a shot of Viagra. His cock jerked awake and rose for another round.

I loved the feeling of opening your pussy, of thrusting through the barrier, of taking what was mine. I still love the memory of your tight virginal walls opening for my cock. You'll never know the touch of another man, and I've wanted a virgin bride my entire life. You're mine. All mine.

"Um, you should probably make that call before she finds out from someone else." She slid down his body until her feet hit the floor. "Where do I go?"

"My bedroom is where you'll sleep from now on. We'll have to get used to sharing our space. We'll move your belongings in here tomorrow. The bedroom you've been sleeping in has to become a guest room again by three o'clock tomorrow afternoon, per our law."

I have to prove we're sleeping in the same bed, or I'll be under investigation by the elders and priests. Not that I'd let you sleep in another bed. You're mine, and everyone will know it by the end of the week.

The bag the church had left at the house for him with his clothes and belongings sat on the top of his dresser. "There should be a white bag for you either hanging on a hook or lying on the counter in the bathroom. The church gathers our belongings for us and brings them to the house so we have no distractions on the drive, or when we arrive home."

While he rifled through the bag and found his cell-phone, she walked into the bathroom.

"Found it," she said. "I'm going to clean up a little."

You're giving me the privacy I don't really need. You're naturally kind and respectful. I don't want to screw up any more than I already have.

"Okay. I'll be quick." He dialed Riley. *Please don't answer. Let me leave a message. I don't want to talk to you tonight.*

"Logan, are you coming over?" Riley answered. "I could really use a good fuck and to talk. That testing was..." She exhaled long and hard. "You told me it was intense and intrusive for non-virgins, but I had no idea it would delve into the darkest parts of my life, too. I see why so few people have perfect matches."

"I'm not coming—"

"Of course you're not. It was stupid of me to ask. It's past curfew. You've got Aurora at the house who is the talk of the town. All the guys are walking around with boners because of her. She is crazy beautiful. All that blonde hair and her hourglass figure. She's a natural blonde bombshell. Is she disappointed about not matching with anyone? I had a partial match with some guy in Georgia, but I haven't contacted him, yet. I'm not sure I want to move. I'm not sure that I could move and continue improving my life like I have here. I might not contact him at all. So, when can I see you again?"

"I'm married. I was a perfect match with—"

"Zinnia. You matched with that Zinnia chick with the long legs and sexy voice. I knew it. Dang it. I'm so pissed. Is she listening? Tell her I still think she's a bitch."

"Not her."

"Gina?"

"No. I matched with—"

"Pamela? Big tits Pamela will show you a good time. I like her. She's open to—"

"I married Aurora. She was a one hundred percent perfect match with me in every way, even the variants."

Silence held the space for far too long.

"You know who and what I am, Riley." *I've had to enforce the law with you too many times for you not to know I'm not human. You're doing well now. You haven't had a slip up in more than a year. Keep on the right path. Don't let this be an excuse to veer off the road of righteousness onto another dark path.*

"She's so young," Riley mumbled. "If she needs anything, please, have her ask me. I'll help her any way I can. She's going to have to memorize the rules of the church and learn about your position as the law in town and in the church."

"Yeah. Thanks, Riley. I was hoping you'd understand."

"I do," she said. "Thank you for calling and telling me before I heard it from someone else. I guess I should take a trip to Georgia, huh?"

"Ask if the man will come here to visit you," he advised. "He might love it here."

Riley wouldn't do well living outside this community. She'd slip up and go down the path she'd walked a hundred times already. She'd take her husband down that path, too. She needed this community, which was why God sent her here. She needed our church. He didn't want her to do something stupid and end up back in prison, having lost her chance to return here to rehabilitate.

"Can I request him to consider moving here?" she asked.

"Yes. I believe he will come for you. Show him around our town. Make an appointment for the two of you to have counseling with the priest. Both of you will know if it will work by the end of the first session. But tell him about the special testing he'd have to go through to join our congregation. Just because he's a member of our sister church does not mean he will be compatible with our church."

"You mean with *your* unbending rules for our church and community," she said.

"Yes. Exactly. Good luck."

"Thanks. Good luck yourself. You're going to need it more than I will." She ended the call.

"Everything go okay?" Aurora asked.

Kind of. She's not as fine with this as she says she is.

He placed the phone down and turned toward her.

Standing near the bed wearing a pink T-shirt and matching pajama shorts, she trembled slightly.

"She said that if you need anything to call her," he said. "She doesn't filter her words well, so they come out harsh more often than not, but deep down, she is soft and cares." At least he hoped she cared. He wouldn't know for sure until he saw her or felt a shift to evil in the energy of the community.

He crossed the room toward Aurora, but she retreated, maneuvering to the other side of the bed, probably searching for some sign to show her where he wanted her to go. The need to dominate her allowed a little enjoyment in her confusion and avoidance of him.

"Thank her for me." Her back hit the hallway wall with a soft thud. "There was a note in the bag. It didn't say anything about pajamas, so I grabbed some from my room."

"This is your room now. It's *our* room. The note didn't have instructions for wearing pajamas because you're not supposed to wear them to bed. Unless you or I have a doctor's note stating we're sick or shouldn't have sex. Or it is mandated within the church rules stating we can't have sex, which is a mandate that is so rare, I haven't seen nor heard one ever being issued."

"Oh. Uh. What do I do?"

The innocence in her question was real. There was no game being played. There was no deceitfulness in her actions. The white of her aura and the pink and red mixture of desire showed him that she wasn't scared of him. But, she was scared of her desires.

"Undress. Fold your clothes and place them on top of the dresser."

"I can put them back in my...um...I can put them back

in the guest room until tomorrow, if you'd prefer them hidden."

"No. You'll place them on top of the dresser. We're not going to hide things between us. We're going to be honest. There will be no secrets in our marriage."

She slid her shorts down and he inhaled to keep control. The woman undressing while he watched was his. All. His.

While she lifted the matching T-shirt over her head, he felt like a caged beast about to be let loose to conquer her body. Yeah, he was going to make love to her in every possible way he could until the morning arrived.

She walked on trembling legs to the dresser, then folded her clothes and left them in a neat pile on top.

"Get in bed," he ordered.

Swiftly, she scurried across the room and climbed into his bed, slipped under the covers.

"This side?" she asked. "I can sleep anywhere. I slept next to my mom a lot, switching back and forth from one side to the other, depending whether my dad was in bed with us or not."

"Either side is good." He joined her in bed. Whether it was the fear she expressed because of the situation or the need to have her soft, pliable body beneath him, he gave her no space in the bed. He crawled to her, halting and hovering over her body. With his knees, he nudged her legs apart and dropped his pelvis. His cock had a mind of its own, it was so hard and hungry and ready to be inside her. He shifted forward, pushing the head of his cock inside her deliciously juicy pussy.

She gasped. "I'm kind of sore."

"Kind of?" he asked. "Are you too sore for sex? Do I

need to call the doctor?" He felt like a jerk, asking her so harshly, but he was hanging on by a thread. He wanted her and he wanted her now.

"I'm kind of sore, but not too sore for, uh…I'm a little scared. It'a all so new. And then at the church there were all those tubes and tests. And there were some in the bag in the bathroom. Um, I wasn't sure if I should've…Um, but I did…I'm ovulating."

If that was her attempt at deterring him from sex, she picked the wrong topic. He was ready for children. Knowing his sperm could fertilize one of her eggs sent his desires soaring. He couldn't hold back any longer. He thrust deep inside her. "You did the tests they added in the bag, while I was on the phone?"

"Yes," she whimpered. "The strips of paper turned green. I'm in the middle of—"

"Bless this," he groaned. "You feel so good…" He gripped the top metal spindle of his headboard. "I'm gonna get you pregnant, Aurora." He hadn't meant to manhandle her or be so bold with his words. Heck, he hadn't meant to take what he wanted, but he did. He rocked back, sat up, and flipped her over. Gripping her ass, he lifted her hips and drove deep inside her pussy.

She gasped, but she didn't fight him. She surrendered to his desires, which only increased his need to claim her —body and soul.

With his right hand, he reached under her and rubbed her clit.

"Logan," she moaned. Her pussy clenched around his cock so hard, he nearly came. But he didn't. Her juices gushed and her pussy made the most glorious sucking noises. She shuddered and shouted into the pillow while her juicy hole welcomed him with each and every stroke of his cock.

He let go, taking his pleasure now that he'd given his wife hers. One thrust and he pumped cum into her pussy, then flipped her onto her back and shoved his cock into her again and released the rest of his cum, filling her up with his seed.

Seeing her flushed body and glistening hole made him instantly hard. Waiting for her to recover wasn't an option, not tonight. He claimed her pussy again, slammed his cock into her.

The more she gasped, the rougher and more demanding he became, until the rush of power burst into a cosmic light show as their auras connected as one, and they found bliss together.

As reality of the earthly world pulled him back from the beauty of sex within marriage, he gazed at her. *You're mine.*

"If you're too sore for sex, you have to tell me. I'll call for the doctor to examine you. It's not unusual for the doctor to make a visit with newlyweds."

She nodded. "Can we sleep for a while? I'm exhausted."

He dropped to his side, facing her. "Yeah. Sleep sounds good." He rolled onto his back.

Within a few minutes, she slid her arm over his chest and fell fast asleep.

Closing his eyes, he tried to ignore the ache in his cock to get inside her again. He'd have to teach her to trust her instincts. He'd have to give her an opportunity to explore his body, to memorize his taste, to listen for the slight changes in his tone to alert her to follow a rule she was close to breaking. He had his work cut out for him, and he wondered when she'd confess her secret. He wasn't sure what exactly she was hiding, but if the truth didn't come out soon, he'd have to punish her.

No one was above the law.

Not him.

Not Aurora.

Not anyone.

CHAPTER ELEVEN

Aurora

The priest hadn't lied when he said that she and Logan would have an early morning. Logan woke up before the rooster crowed and started his chores, while he graciously allowed her to sleep. Not that she remained in bed long. He sent her a text with a list of tasks to be done before he returned. She rolled out of bed, tired and aware of all the places he'd touched her.

After making the bed and taking a quick shower, she started with the first item on the to-do list which was moving her belongings into his room and taking the dirty clothes and sheets into the laundry room. She tidied up as she finished one task in a room and started on a new task in another room.

Logan popped into the house, washed his hands, and wrapped her up in his arms, giving her a bunch of sweet kisses. Then he dropped the bomb that Riley, his ex-girl-friend, was outside, dropping off a few product orders, and picking up some furniture he'd made for one of her clients.

While Aurora smiled and nodded at his explanations as to why his ex-girlfriend had shown up at seven-thirty in the morning the day after his wedding, she used every tool in her emotional toolbox and succeeded in pushing away the jealousy knocking on her soul to be let in.

"Have you checked to see if you're still ovulating?" he asked.

And that one question quelled her worry about his possible continued interest in Riley. He wanted to start a family with Aurora, not Riley. He might still have reserva-tions over her young age, but he wanted her pregnant with his child. And the electricity crackling in the air all around her felt like a sign of his desire to take her to bed again.

"Yes, sir. I followed the instructions on the note from the priest and took the tests. I am still ovulating."

He curled his arm around her and pulled her against his chest, forcing her to arch her back to see those blue eyes that made her feel all warm and gooey inside.

"Aurora, I can't stop thinking about you, about touching you, making love to you. I want you beside me all the time."

The joy that filled her with his honest words made up for the sudden arrival of his ex-girlfriend.

"Same," she whispered. "You could've asked me to help move the furniture into the bedroom. I could do it now."

"I had planned to move everything in myself, but she

showed up, unannounced, for the other furniture and offered to help for the inconvenience. We'll move it as soon as her delivery guys have the other pieces in their truck. She wants to meet you, although I'd rather keep you naked in my bed. No visitors allowed." He kissed her forehead and nose and lips. "I'm not going to be happy until I get you back in our bed and all the visitors who will be coming to the house this afternoon and this week are gone."

"Then get back to your list of things we need to get done, and I'll continue working on the list you gave me, so you can take off all my clothes and make love to me."

When he didn't move from holding her, she looked for any signs that his desire for her had turned addictive or dangerous. Not finding any darkness in his aura, she determined that the analysis of her testing in the church for matchmaking must also test for supernatural gifts like hers. But the entire church body held no reaction to her touch. The priests and parishioners seemed immune to the addictive qualities she'd become accustomed to experiencing from regular interactions from people wherever she lived. Maybe their lack of a reaction was because she was with Logan. The man had the brightest and strongest white aura she'd ever seen. She'd never heard of one man counteracting the addiction that occurred from people touching her, but she didn't know much about gifts that other people had. She didn't know the extent of her own gifts and couldn't wager to guess the kind of gifts Logan might have.

Maybe God had made the congregation safe from any addiction her greeting might induce. Logan had told her the church here was different, that the community was different. Even though the township was in the State of Texas, Exorcise was its own country—part of God's promised land of refuge for those who seek it. She was skeptical of God's hand in building this town in order to set it apart as His special place, but since arriving only a couple days ago, her life had changed. She didn't want to leave this community, this town, this land. And she hoped that Logan planned to live here forever.

While she thought about the town and wondered why Logan continued to hold her and stare into her eyes, fears of having to leave this place pushed her to ask him about his future plans. Since he worked for the church, she pondered whether he planned to seek a position at a national level within the church hierarchy. If he did want to rise to a high position in the church, he might eventually need to transfer to a sister church. Possibly move to where the national church was located. He might want to branch out and spend time at an international church within the denomination? Would he choose to stay here in his current job forever? Would he be happy if he remained here because she wanted to stay? Would he consider asking her opinion about moving?

"I've, uh, never had a home, like a permanent home," she confessed. "You don't plan to sell this place, do you? All the changes that the church is having us make this week isn't to sell the house and move somewhere else, right?"

He shook his head. "I was born here. I grew up in this house. This land has been in my family for more generations than I can count. My family sold the land in town to the founders of the church. I own a lot of property in this county. When you look all around you, the land you see is mine. It's ours. This is your home now. We might make additions onto the house, but we're *never* selling or abandoning our home."

"Okay," she said. "But if you do ever go anywhere, don't leave me. Take me with you."

"Darlin', you're mine. Where I go, you'll go. But this is *our home*. This is *our town*. We might take a trip to visit someone or take a vacation somewhere, but *we always come home*."

"Okay," she said. *That's a relief.* "I'll be in the laundry room while you get that armoire moved."

"I'll have Riley out of here quickly." He made a growly, grumble of a noise. "I'm not a fan of this part of the marriage laws."

"Same." She reached around her back and ignored the spark that accompanied the moment she touched his hands. Curling her fingers around his, she stepped backward and eased his hands from around her. "You told me it's important that the house is prepared for guests in a certain way. I'd like to follow the rules and make a good impression on your friends."

While she straightened and pulled her black tank top to cover her belly, he stepped forward and cupped her cheeks. "You are perfect." He kissed her lips and held her hands once more. "I've got to double check my workspace for any other pieces they might have missed for her clients. Then I'll get that armoire in here in a few minutes, so I can help you put away the clean clothes."

"That list you texted me has shopping for decorative

pillows and rugs, dishes and fine china," she said. "I don't know how we're going to get all that done."

"We'll get it done," he assured her. He slid his freshly shaved cheek against hers and grumbled something, then dipped his head and kissed her neck. "You look beautiful today. I want you right now."

"Stop stalling and maybe you'll get me as soon as we're done," she whispered.

"Maybe?" He brushed her hair over her shoulder and continued kissing down her neck.

She smiled and leaned into his kisses. "I'm a sure thing, Logan. But your ex-girlfriend is here and so are her delivery men. Until they're all gone, absolutely nothing intimate will happen."

His kisses ended, which she wanted but also didn't want. "She's not my ex-girlfriend. She was never my girl-friend. But we'll have to argue about that later." He dropped her hands and stepped back. His hand went to what looked like a painfully large bulge in his jeans. "The minute she's gone, I'm going to—"

"Logan, finish with them. I'll be here when you get back." *Hurry and get everyone out of the house. I want you all to myself.*

"Fine." He exhaled, pivoted, and was out the door, moving faster than seemed humanly possible. In fact, he seemed to be faster and stronger than any man she'd ever met. The more she thought about last night...and not the sexy parts, which were most of the parts...

She squeezed her thighs together, crossing her legs and sucking in her breath. Just the thought of making love to him made her panties wet. Being with him made her forget about every bad thing that ever happened to her. In this house, in *his* house, she was safe and surrounded by God's light of protection. If Logan was her perfect match, and she believed he was, then he had to have some kind of gift from God, like she did with healing.

While she walked through the house into the laundry room off the kitchen, she thought of the possibility that Logan's gift was protecting people. He had served in the armed forces, and came back to be the sheriff in town, which would support the assumption that God gifted him with the ability to protect people who needed it. But he also said that he would judge and punish those he found who broke the law. Something about a person being both judge and jury seemed questionable. What person, left to their own devices, would be able to consistently dole out ethical judgments and punishments without once choosing selfishly? Someone had to have at least tried to bribe him, probably more people offered him bribes than she could imagine. He'd have to be otherworldly, possibly supernatural, possibly someone with angel blood, like her to avoid that kind of temptation.

But if he had angel blood, he'd be in danger like her. The man went all over the world and no one seemed to be chasing him. Sure, women swooned around him. Gosh, every woman in town gave him a second or third, or more realistically a fourth glance. She might not like it, but she couldn't blame them. He was some serious eye candy. He touched people all the time and no one seemed to react strangely. But this town was different. No one reacted strangely to her random touch, except Logan. And she reacted so strongly to Logan's touch, she struggled to tear herself away. Maybe he did cause people to have an addiction to him.

Without a second to spare, she made a beeline to the bedroom to fold the clean clothes she added to the white laundry basket. She wasn't allowing his ex-girlfriend into the bedroom without her being present. No way. No how.

CHAPTER TWELVE

Aurora

While gorgeous Riley Riesling helped Logan move an armoire from his workshop in the barn into his bedroom, Aurora held a laundry basket. She hated the fact that she looked more like a daughter instead of a wife. Nothing about her looked like she belonged to Logan or he to her. Logan didn't look his age, but he didn't look like a teenager either. The more she stared at him and Riley, the more she thought they seemed like they were the couple in the room. And that fact riled Aurora up more than she ever wanted to admit.

The long-haired brunette flipped her hair over her shoulder and seductively smiled at him. "We can hang the mirror you made on the wall above your headboard, not that there's much of a decent headboard, but it will look good there."

"I made that headboard," he mumbled.

"I love the headboard. It's the most beautiful bed I've ever seen," Aurora whispered, gazing at him. Even though she spoke quietly, she gazed into his blue eyes and the tenderness in his eyes and smile assured her that he'd heard her.

"Aurora, what do you think?" Riley glanced at her, her mouth in an open smile as if she hadn't just flirted with Logan.

"I'll hang the mirror later," Logan said.

"Fine." Riley rolled her eyes. "Aurora, want to come to my boutique and pick out some throw pillows and décor? Logan sucks at the finishing touches in a room. He can build and upholster anything, but curtains and pillows seem to terrify the man." She playfully squeezed his arm. "Isn't that right?"

I don't want you touching my husband like that. You want him. I don't think being alone with you is a good idea. You'll end up bullying me, and I don't want to deal with that.

"I'm not terrified of anything," Logan grumbled.

"Logan," Aurora asked softly. "Will you come with me?" There was no way she'd leave without him, at least, not with Riley.

"Yeah. Sure," he replied. "I'll drive."

"He's got chores to do," Riley said. "While he's working, you can drive his truck. We'll decide what to add to the house and you can bring it all back here."

Staring at Logan, she pleaded with her eyes. *Please tell her that you're taking me. I'm jealous of her. She's jealous of me. I need you to take control. You need to stop her from—*

"Aurora will help me with the chores when we get back," Logan said. "Let's go and get the pillows and stuff."

"She's an adult, Logan. She can do this alone. *She doesn't need you,*" Riley insisted. "She made it here from Georgia, driving *all by herself.* She can survive an hour or two *without you.*"

"And I can drive her and help pick out what we need, cutting whatever time it takes in half. That'll give me enough time to hang whatever I need to hang and get the chores done before everyone starts arriving," Logan stated. "My wife stays with me, Riley."

"I hate this side of you," Riley growled. "You're such a controlling asshole sometimes."

"I'm a controlling man *all* the time," Logan said. "Get in the truck, Riley. And don't try and intimidate my wife into doing something she's not comfortable doing, because *she did recently arrive* here. And *she doesn't know you.*"

"It's not like I'm going to hurt her," Riley huffed. "She's got to learn to do things on her own. Get to town on her own. Shop on her own. Make her *own* friends." She grunted and puffed out harsh exhales as she crossed the room to Aurora. "You have to learn to stand up to him. You're never going to make it in this town cowering under his every demand."

Aurora stepped backward, avoiding the confrontation, and silently pleading for Logan's help. *I need you.*

"She's not cowering, Riley. She's obeying me. I know what she needs." Logan swooped in and took the basket from Aurora's hands, facing her and blocking Riley from her view. "Riley has strong opinions, sweetheart. She's not attacking you. She's trying to give you advice. It's *bad* advice that you will *not* follow."

"It's okay. I can see she loves you." *It's so not okay.* Aurora took the basket from his hands.

She's head over heels in love with you. She's trying to prove that I'm too young and naïve and weak for a man like you. That you can't love someone like me. Can you love me? Do you love me? Would you love me?

"It's not okay," Logan said softly. "Do you want to go to Riley's boutique? If it's too much, tell me."

"I don't want to spend money we don't have to on things we don't need. You've spent too much on me already." She didn't want him to resent her. Money didn't seem like an issue to him, but it had been a major issue in her life. They never had enough and her father always wanted more, spending what they had on bets that always had him losing more than he had. Logan had a nice home and he didn't need to buy stuff they didn't need.

"We're going to Riley's Boutique and picking out a few things," Logan ordered. "Put down the basket and let's go now. I want you to show me what you like. Don't look at the price tag." He glanced over his shoulder. "Riley, don't tell her what anything costs. I'll take care of that privately."

"Okay," Riley mumbled.

Logan turned his head toward her and took the basket from Aurora's hands again, placing it on the bed.

"Is it important that the house be decorated so quickly?" Aurora asked. She didn't understand the rush to get everything done. Don't most people go on honeymoons after the wedding? What do they do?

"Yes. We need to decorate immediately," Logan said. "Our house reflects my tastes. It needs to reflect *our* tastes.

Every aspect of our home carries with it the rules of the church. A welcoming comes first and our house has to reflect that it is ours, not mine or yours. The kitchen and bathrooms take a little longer to make renovations, so we have two weeks to decide on and acquire those items before we're allowed to go out of town on a honeymoon." He pulled her into his arms. "If you see something for the kitchen today, we can buy it. And I'm sure you're thinking about the money and how other couples manage the church's rules on a budget. The church has funds for those who need it. We support all members and those who live in our town, regardless of financial circumstances. We don't make rules so that people can't follow them. We make it so that *everyone* has the opportunity to obey them. It is their choice whether to adhere to the rules, or face the consequences."

She slid her hands under his black T-shirt and glided over the thick muscles of his lower back. *I like your church more and more.* "I can't promise I'll pick anything out for the kitchen or bathroom, but I'll think about it."

I want to go on that honeymoon. I want to be alone with you. No visitors. No interruptions. No courtrooms. No crimes. No demons. Only you and me.

"Please, do it for me. If you see anything you like, I want you to have it." He gripped her butt and hoisted her up so fast she caught air before she landed in his arms and wrapped her legs around his waist.

Is this why those ceilings are so high? You planned to play "who can toss their wife up in the air the highest"?

He kissed her cheek. "Don't worry. You're safe. Don't think about the call this morning. We'll go to Atlanta together. I won't let anything happen to you."

Pulling her lower lip into her mouth, she held it

tightly, biting down, so she wouldn't start crying. She hadn't thought about the call from the prosecutor since it happened. He'd done an excellent job in making her forget that she needed to be in Atlanta next week to testify. They might not have two weeks to prepare the bathrooms and kitchen to stay in compliance with the church rules. She needed to make decisions today, not tomorrow or next week.

The call alerting her that the court had fast-tracked the case and she was needed in court next week to testify came as a shock. She hadn't expected the District Attorney to move so quickly. In the past two years, nothing had moved quickly in the judicial system, especially not with the criminal in question. In fact, the prosecution seemed to turn a blind eye when the man who assaulted and tried to kidnap her walked into the courtroom for his arraignments, only sentencing the man short stints in jail.

But now, the man had made such a spectacle out of what he'd done to her parents, the prosecution team suddenly decided to move at warp speed with the case. When Logan took the phone from her hand and spoke with the lead prosecutor, he listened for what seemed like forever. In the end, Logan agreed to bring Aurora to Georgia to prepare and then give her testimony—a testimony she wasn't ready to give. She wasn't ready to face the man who murdered her parents. She didn't want to talk to the prosecution who were probably working for him, taking bribes, doing whatever they could to get her back in Atlanta to give to that evil man. Logan couldn't protect her there. No one could protect her there.

"Aurora, please, don't cry," he whispered.

"I won't." But she did. Tears trickled down her cheeks the more she thought about why they were in such a time crunch to get the house ready for inspection. He upheld the law and set the example for everyone else to follow. And being his wife, she also had to stand beside him as an example of a model citizen. She might not know all the laws or the extent of Logan's role as Sheriff, but she did know his job was important. She had the nipple rings to remind her. "I'm sorry."

She ran her hands over her face and wiped away the tears, pulling her emotions back under control. Logan promised to protect her wherever she might be in the world. As long as they were together, she had nothing to fear. And she believed him. She trusted him. "Let's go get those pillows. Maybe a duvet or comforter or quilt or something in white or something in a light color. Maybe another couch and a chair or two for the living room?"

"Choose anything you want. We're perfectly matched, which means I will love whatever you pick out." He kissed under her ear and spoke so quietly only she could hear. "We better go before I strip you naked and make love to you for the rest of the afternoon."

That dried up all her tears and sent heat waves through her that lingered in the places he explored last night and this morning.

"I love you," she whispered, speaking the words she'd held back because they were still virtually strangers. It had only been a couple days since they met, but she felt like they'd been together since the beginning of time. Except there stood Riley, interfering in their relationship. No matter how much she loved him, Riley loved him, first. And no matter how much he denied it, he had feelings for the woman. It might not be love, but it *was* something.

"I love you so much, Aurora."

She doubted his words of love, but when she searched his aura and gazed into his eyes, she saw a love so strong it nearly toppled her over. She'd never felt nor seen anything like it. Not between two people. Her father and mother loved each other, but not like what she saw in Logan's aura.

In that moment, she knew Logan had some angel blood flowing through his veins, or he'd never have been a match to her with all the strict guidelines and testing in the church. The man was stronger and more steadfast than her mother had ever been, and her mother was a real angel—an angel who fell in love with a broken Hell-bound man.

She swung her legs down while he held her, preventing her from falling. *I can do this. You love me. I have to trust that you really do love me, NOT Riley. I need to trust your word and your aura. I need to trust my instincts and the church's matchmaking program. Most of all I need to trust God and believe in my heart that I'm right where I'm supposed to be, following His will for my life.*

He lowered her, pressing her against his big bulge on her way down. While he held her, he pivoted to face Riley. "We're ready."

The beautiful brunette swallowed hard and the gray hues of disappointment leaking from beneath the thin layer of white light around her were slowly snuffed out by the pinks and reds of love as she gazed at Logan. "Let's go. We should stop in and shop at a couple of the stores near mine, too. We'll be in and out in forty-five minutes."

Logan strode forward, gently, yet firmly, tugging Aurora along beside him. "We'll drop you off home when we're done."

"That would be great," Riley mumbled.

You may be in love with Logan, but he's mine.

Aurora grasped Riley's hand as she stepped onto the porch, attempting to change Riley's focus. She hoped that the woman was like everyone else in this town—strangely unaffected by Aurora's presence. "Thanks for your help."

While Riley closed the front door and squeezed Aurora's hand, the pinks and reds of love shifted to grays and murky greens. "It's the least I can do."

The woman looked Aurora up and down as she let go of Aurora's hand. The darker colors of Riley's aura shifted once more, lightening the colors until they were fully snuffed out by the powerful white light radiating from Logan's spirit. The man's purity of spirit seemed to permeate into Riley until her aura morphed to white, not as vibrant a white as Logan's but a lesser version that was oddly similar to the others in the community.

Riley pulled on her boots. With a curve of her lips into a sexy smile, she slid her hands up her legs and glanced at Logan.

He's not looking at you…But I am. I know what you're doing and it's wrong.

Riley's smile faded as her gaze dipped down to Aurora's. "You're just a kid," she mumbled. "You're going to crumble under all his rules."

Acting like she didn't hear Riley, Aurora stepped closer to Logan and slipped her feet into the new boots Logan bought her.

I've got to stop overanalyzing her aura. She loves him. He's lovable. He's gorgeous and brilliant. But he says that he loves me. I don't know how he could love me. I'm a complete hot mess. And Miss Gorgeous Riley, you're not helping me gain any confidence. And part of me truly thinks you want to help me. But all of me believes you're only doing this to impress my husband, who you can't have. Logan is mine. He is mine and the sooner you realize it, the better.

During the short walk to the truck, Logan grabbed Aurora's hand and pulled her close enough to him that he gave her sweet pecks on the cheek with each few steps. He opened the driver side of the truck and lifted Aurora up into the cab. "Scoot into the middle so Riley can sit up here, too."

Before Aurora could object, Riley climbed in the passenger side, sandwiching Aurora in the middle. While Aurora tried to think of ways to avoid the woman's fluctuating aura and attitude toward her, Aurora tried to take up as much room as possible to force Riley into the backseat. But Riley buckled her seatbelt and stretched out, forcing Aurora to accept the fact that Riley wasn't going anywhere. Aurora couldn't ignore the woman. She had to face her and try to befriend her, if for no other reason than to keep the church's rule to treat others as special gifts from God. Maybe one day she could heal Riley of her heartbreak over Logan.

Logan slid into his seat and buckled Aurora in before he snapped his seatbelt in place.

The engine roared to life. Logan quickly drove down the driveway as the wheels kicked up the white rocks and sent them flying behind the truck. Logan stopped at the end of the drive and gazed at Aurora, then turned onto the main road toward town. His hand on her thigh inched upward until it was snug between her legs.

Aurora's parents never touched each other when they were in public. No handholding or kisses on the cheek. No private whispers. Dad's hand never touched her mother in public, not even on her back to guide her through a door. But Logan didn't hold back his affection, whether it was holding hands or touching her leg or kissing her lips or cheek. When Logan wanted to touch Aurora, he did. The platonic snuggles and hugs he'd given her prior to last night had changed to hugs and snuggles that always led to kisses and sex and more sex. Not that she was complaining, but it was different than what she'd grown up seeing from her parents. It was a lovely difference. One of her favorite parts of being his wife.

He leaned over and kissed her cheek. "I want you," he whispered.

She curled her arms around his. "You have me."

"Not the way I want," he grumbled. His hand on the steering wheel squeezed a little tighter. He didn't seem to want to go shopping either.

"Can you leave the girl alone for two seconds?" Riley huffed.

"No," Logan said. "I can't."

"You were never like that with me," she mumbled.

That one confession from her told her that Riley had been in love with Logan for a long time, while his romantic feelings for her were superficial while they were together.

"*She's my wife*, Riley," he said. "I love her, and I want everyone to know *she's mine*."

The strength and tone in his words had Aurora leaning

closer to him, relishing his statements. She loved his possessiveness and she wondered if it was because she felt the same. Or it could have been that he'd stood up to Riley, reminding her that their relationship was over and his with Aurora was forever. From what Aurora could tell, Riley didn't give up easily, and this wouldn't be the only time Logan would tell Riley the blunt truth. Logan didn't sugar coat anything.

"You know I'm yours," Aurora replied. "Isn't that enough?"

"No. It's not enough," he stated. "By the end of the day, every person in our congregation, all members within our sister churches, along with our entire community will know you're my wife. And even then, it won't be enough."

"You're smothering her," Riley said. "She's going to rebel against your authority."

"My wife is not smothered, nor is her well-being yours to be concerned with," he replied. "My wife will obey the law like I obey the law. *She's. Not. You.*"

"Uh, is it always this hot in Texas?" Aurora tried to change the subject—which seemed to be centered around her.

"Yes," Riley said. "It's *hot as Hell* in Exorcise, Texas. Logan and his grandfather love the heat. They love the dust. They love working the land and caring for the animals. You're going to see first-hand how their presence or absence affects the people and the land and the animals of Exorcise, Texas. You're in for an education, young lady."

"I like the heat," Aurora said. "Do you like it, Riley?"

"No," Riley said. "I like the people here. I like the way the town was built. I like that there is no crime and the people who settle here have to agree to the laws or they have to leave. There are no exceptions to signing the community contract with all their rules. I like the affluence within the community, and that the descendants of the family who founded this town are still involved in its governance to continue the community's slow and steady growth. You're not going to like it here, Aurora. You're used to big cities where no one knows you. This is a small town where everyone knows everybody and all of their personal business."

Aurora held onto Logan a little tighter. The woman didn't want her with Logan or in this town. She wanted Logan all to herself, and Aurora couldn't blame her one bit. The man was as perfect as a man could ever be. Tall, handsome, and strong. Not an ounce of fat on the man. He was built with muscle upon muscle. And in those dark denim jeans that hugged his ass and thighs...*Mmm.*

"Small town life is not easy and you're a big city girl. You're going to *hate it here.*" Riley seemed to growl as she spoke. Her mouth flattened to a scowl.

The hostility from Riley pushed against Aurora, attempting to infiltrate Aurora's aura.

Aurora pushed back, driving the gray and murky green muddled spiritual sludge away as Logan's presence fought back, strengthening and removing the remnants that clung to the edges.

Do you know your aura battles evil thoughts of other people? Is your expansive and strong spirit the reason there is no crime here? Are you aware of your ability to protect me from Riley, while protecting Riley from herself?

"Don't worry," Logan whispered. "You're going to love it here. We're a perfect match in every way. Soon we'll be building an addition onto the house for our future children."

Aurora raised her gaze to his and smiled. *I want babies who look just like you.*

"You better get used to him taking a shower as soon as he's done fucking you. No cuddles. Nothing but his satisfaction matters. Other men aren't like him," Riley nearly shouted. "Other men *care* about whether their lover gets an orgasm or not."

Logan's brows rose as he glanced at her. "I'll drop you off at your house. Aurora and I will shop elsewhere."

"Oh my God, that's so fucking like you," Riley fumed. "No. I'll keep my mouth shut. *Your wife* will have to experience all your bullshit on her own. I won't warn her or tell her what to do."

"You need to spend the rest of the drive thinking about the lies you tell, the language you use, and how you're going to handle the rest of our time together."

"Got it," Riley grunted.

Aurora wasn't sure but she thought she heard a "fuck you" under Riley's breath. From the look Logan gave her, Aurora thought he might've heard it, too.

"You have choices, Riley," Logan said. "And there are consequences to those choices. If you're not capable of making the right choice, then I will enforce the law and dole out your sentence."

"Yes, *sir*," Riley mumbled. She flipped her long hair over her shoulder, the tresses smacking Aurora in her face. "Logan, you're such a—"

"Control yourself, Riley," Logan stated. He cut her off, and pulled Aurora closer to him. "Do not listen to her, Aurora. She's throwing a tantrum."

Riley huffed and pursed her full red lips. Even angry, she was beautiful. Tall and lean, highlighted by her expensive skinny jeans and emerald green T-shirt that matched her eyes and drew the eye to her perky, surgically augmented breasts. The woman liked to argue and she had a harsh tongue. She liked to control others, especially those who disliked confrontation. She and Aurora had virtually nothing in common, except their love for Logan. Aurora hoped that with Logan's help, she might be able to find a way to heal Riley's anger. She focused on blocking Riley's influence by envisioning God's white light of healing infiltrating Riley's aura.

CHAPTER THIRTEEN

Aurora

While Riley seethed in silence next to Aurora, Logan seemed unfazed with Riley's outburst. He just focused on the road and inching Aurora closer to him.

While Logan drove past the first building in the town square, he shoved his hand down his jeans and adjusted his bulge. Then he placed his hand on Aurora's thigh and slid it up, resting against her sex. The way his hand rubbed between her legs, gently parting her pussy lips and circling the tight bud, made her embarrassingly wet. She turned toward him and crossed her leg, attempting to pin his hand down so it would stop moving in ways to arouse her. If he didn't stop soon, her desire would seep through her jeans. She wanted him just as much as he wanted her, but Riley stretched and pressed her side against Aurora's.

Logan gazed at Aurora with a sexy look that melted her into an agreeing and obedient mess, which was sure to get Riley angry enough to start talking again. He seemed so socially unaware of Riley's presence that he kissed across her cheek to her ear. "I want to spread you out naked on our bed and lick every inch of you."

Without thinking, Aurora turned her head toward him, catching a taste of his tongue and lips.

As if on cue to block the intimate moment, Riley opened her mouth. "Take a right. You're not paying any attention to where you're going."

"I know exactly where I am." Logan glanced at the road and took a right, parking in front of Riley's Home Boutique. He unsnapped Aurora's seatbelt and was out of the truck in an instant, sliding her across the bench seat into his arms. With a quick kiss on her lips, he let gravity lower her against his hard body until her boots landed softly on the ground. He shut the door and led her toward the entrance to Riley's shop, without even a slight glance at the beautiful brunette.

Not to be outmaneuvered by Logan, Riley exited the car and scampered to the front door, scooting in front of them before they reached the door. She unlocked and held open the tempered glass door with the shop's name on it. But Logan reached over her head and took hold of the door from her, taking control.

"Go on in, ladies," Logan said with an undertone of an order.

Riley huffed, but stepped inside, and Aurora followed her.

Logan crossed the threshold, bathing the store in his

pure white light, and closed the door. "The place looks great. You rearranged the showrooms."

"Yep." Riley sashayed through the sections and pointed out things that would look good in Logan's house, periodically gazing at Aurora.

Logan picked up a cream-colored, suede pillow with light pink suede fringe. "This seems like it represents you, Aurora. Do you like it?"

"I do, but not for the living room."

Riley picked up a cream-colored leather floor pillow. "Something like this would look good in his living room with the gray couch I helped him pick out two years ago." Then she grabbed a sky blue, velvet couch cushion. "And this."

Aurora nodded. "Yes, ma'am." *I'm aware you've known him for a long time. You're interested in picking out all the little pieces that make a house a home for him. To please him. To remind him of you. I know your game, but I don't care. Logan is mine. He's mine, and nothing you do will change that fact.*

Riley grabbed the pillows and tossed them on a cream-colored leather couch nearby. "Give me ten minutes, and I'll have a few options to spruce up the bedroom and living room."

"I like the cream-colored leather couch," Aurora whispered to Logan. "Maybe you could make one? Can you do that?"

"I made that one," he said. "I can make you anything you want, but it will take some time. Time we don't have right now." He pulled Aurora into the kitchen section, far away from Riley.

As soon as they were alone, his lips crushed hers. His

hands glided along her waist, lifting up her pale pink T-shirt, skimming over her skin, sending sparks through her body. As his hands caressed her hips, she softened more and more against his touch. He slid his hands down the back of her jeans and squeezed her ass. She tried to ignore the desire to strip down to her birthday suit and make love to him, but his demanding touch made it extremely hard.

He lifted her up, seating her on the white granite counter, his hips between her thighs. He thrust his bulge against her sex. "I want to be inside you."

"Not here." *That is one thing I will not do in public, especially in your ex-girlfriend's boutique.* She shouldn't have, but she couldn't stop herself from slipping her hands under his pale blue T-shirt to the smooth skin over hard, defined muscles. "I want you, too. But we can't continue doing this here."

A man-rumble from deep within his chest sent another round of heated shivers through her. "I know we can't," he murmured. *"Uhhgg.* She's making this take much longer than it should. We're perfectly matched, and it's hard for her to understand what that means. I'm sorry I had a relationship with her. The other women I've been with have all understood that it wasn't about love, only a physical need."

A soft gasp filled Aurora's ears. She looked over her right shoulder.

Standing with tears in her eyes and an aura fighting to maintain more white light than gray, Riley held a sky-blue throw in her arms. "This might be nice in—"

Logan growled. "Riley, enough."

Aurora snapped her focus back on him. "She's just—"

He stared into Aurora's eyes. "She's not just being

kind, Aurora. You have five minutes to get whatever we need to make our living room look like ours, *not mine.*" He let go of her and walked to the front door, ignoring the hurt brunette.

"Woah," Riley mumbled.

Aurora hopped off the counter. "I'm sorry about all of that. But, I need to hurry. Can you show me where the living room section is?" She wanted to just leave, but Riley's boutique carried all the home goods in town. There wasn't another option with the lack of time available to get the house together. It was Riley's Home Boutique or Aurora and Logan would break the rules of the church.

While Riley strode to the couch section where she tossed the leather and velvet pillows, Aurora watched Riley's aura shift from a heavier amount of gray than white to a balanced scale of gray and white.

"You need to stand up to him," Riley said.

While Aurora ignored her statement, she eyed a simple, yet beautifully made white silk quilt, stitched with gold and silver threading in a ring pattern, laying over a white couch metal grommet accents in gold.

Aurora pointed to the quilt. "I love that."

"Of course you do," she mumbled. "It's one of a kind and very expensive."

"How much is it?" Aurora asked.

"It's real gold and platinum thread. Do you still want it?"

"No. It's beautiful, though." Aurora walked to the dozens of pillows and picked out some cream pillows with hints of pink in different fabrics—from leather to suede to silk to velvet—to go with the simple cream leather floor pillows. As much as she liked the sky-blue pillows and throws Riley picked out, she took to heart what Logan had said—that the house needed to reflect both of their tastes. She thought a hint of pink might bring enough of her imprint into the house that the congregation would see that the home was now theirs, not only his.

"Logan, come and get the girly pillows Aurora picked out," Riley shouted. "Grab a big bag from beneath the first couch." She grabbed Aurora's hand and led her to a green sofa. "His couch is old and he needs a new one." She pointed to a simple caramel-stained leather sofa across from the cream-colored leather couch Logan made that they sat on. "That one is perfect for the space. I'll call my delivery guy and get it delivered to the house in an hour. I'll bring more décor and stage the room. Anything you *both* like, Logan can purchase. Everything else, I'll bring back to the shop."

"Okay." *That sounds reasonable. You're back to being a professional.*

Logan strode into the room, glanced at Aurora and then the couch. A slight smile crossed his lips as he glanced over the pillows. "Everything on the cream leather couch?"

"Yep," Riley said. "On the floor in front of the couch, too. And you're buying a new sofa—the caramel leather one, lamps, pillows and curtains. I'm adding a chaise and a rug. Anything you don't like once I stage it, I'll take back with me."

"Add that quilt with the gold rings," Logan said. "It's beautiful and looks like something Aurora would like."

Aurora couldn't help but smile. "It's too expensive, but I do love it."

"Riley, I definitely want the quilt," Logan said.

"I'll add it to the delivery," Riley said.

"Am I driving you home?" Logan's gaze drifted at the bags in front of the couch and the slight smile dropped into a flat expression.

Aurora stared at Riley. *You're angry, and he doesn't care. And he's angry, and you don't care.*

"Nope. I'll get the delivery guys to take me over to your place and then home."

"Aurora, come," he shouted.

"Coming," Aurora replied. She was about to run after Logan, but the way Riley stared at her, she remained in place, too scared to move. *De-escalate the situation.*

She looked into Riley's brown eyes. *You're an addict. Darkness chases you. You're dangerous.* "Please, I need to go... He's angry."

"Aurora," Logan shouted. "Come here. Now."

Riley grabbed her arm. "I hope you like being controlled." The low growling undertone of her voice made Aurora tremble.

Logan, help me. I'm scared.

"Riley, please let me go. Logan is calling me." Aurora's heart raced as Riley's grip tightened, bruising her and keeping her in place. There was a darkness inside the woman. A familiar darkness. One like her father's.

God, please let me get away from her.

"Please, Riley, please let me go."

CHAPTER FOURTEEN

Aurora

*L*ogan, *where are you? I need you now.*

"Riley, I'm begging you, please let me go."

She tried to shake her arm free from Riley's strong grip, but the woman was too strong.

"Shit." Riley's mouth gaped.

Logan stomped toward Aurora, as if he'd heard her silent prayer. "Riley Reisling, release my wife," Logan demanded.

Riley's hands shot up in surrender, releasing her grip on Aurora. "It's all good. No need to be upset."

Aurora rushed to him, wrapping her arms around him. *Thank you for coming to my rescue.* "I'm sorry. I'm ready to go."

"Everything is in the car." Logan hugged her and kissed her forehead, then stepped back, breaking the embrace. "When I call you, you come the first time." He turned, taking large strides out of the boutique, toward his truck.

"Yes, sir." She hurried, nearly sprinting to keep up with him.

Once inside the cab of his truck, he cupped the back of her head and stared into her eyes. "You obey me. No one else. Do you understand?"

"Yes, sir," she said. "She grabbed me, and I didn't know what to do. She's older than me. She's really strong." *Evil has a hold of her soul. She needs a cleansing or she's going to attack me. She'll try to kidnap me. I can't heal her alone. I need someone with a pure spirit and a strength of faith that is unshakeable. I need another angel to heal her.*

"I know she's strong, but you have power over her. I have a lot to teach you. But when I order you to do something, *you must obey.* My rules are the law here, so you *must* obey *me* first, everyone else is secondary. You're new, so you're allowed a few corrections without punishment. Who do you obey first?"

"I obey *you* first," she said. "I just didn't want to be disrespectful. And she was hurting me."

"It was Riley who was disrespectful." He kissed her lips. "I saw your confusion and then fear. I felt it inside my spirit, along with your physical pain and your silent pleas for help. Riley can be trouble. She often needs correction." He gently pressed his forehead to hers. "I was so angry with Riley for interrupting us, for delaying you, for testing me." He inhaled and then released her. "But you were never in danger. You have nothing to fear within the county limits. Exorcise is safe, and I am always near. I will *always* save you."

He drove out of the parking spot in front of the store and turned down the main street toward home.

"Will you help me memorize the rules?" she asked. "Teach me how to defend myself?"

"Yes," he said. "If you are keeping any secrets from me, you need to tell me what they are. I don't have any secrets. Riley was a semi-secret, but not really because I didn't hide the fact that we dated from anyone who asked. Not that we really dated. It was more like companionship. But I'm healthy, and haven't been diagnosed with any illnesses other than the common cold, which happened once, when I was a baby, and it was a misdiagnosis. I was in a growth spurt, not unwell."

"I have this thing. Um. My mom and grandmother had it. I heal faster than normal people. I don't get sick. My, uh, my perspiration and body fluids have healing proper-ties. Sometimes, if I'm with the right person, this powerful energy comes over me and a person who is struggling with…" *How do I tell you the full truth?* She exhaled. *You need to know everything. When the demon gets freed from jail, you'll know why I need your protection.*

"If a person is seeking to change their life and embrace good," she said. *I have to tell him everything.* "I can—under the right circumstances—heal their spirit so the darkness flees from them, never to return. Um, those people are rare. Most people only want physical healing. Once healed, any darkness in their spirit that had been there prior to the healing will come back tenfold because their true intentions weren't pure. And other bad things, very bad things, sprout vines from that evil root and expand to those around them."

"I'm familiar with those types of people." He rubbed

his lips together. "Do the nipple rings cause issues with your breasts? I noticed drops of golden fluid coming from the piercings when we make love."

"The fluid is a side-effect of being pierced, but it's fine. The rings are fine." She rubbed her palms against her thighs. "Actually, I like the rings that show I'm your wife. Do you like the rings?"

"Yes, I like the rings," he said. "Do you know what the golden fluid is?"

"It's my body trying to mend through the piercings. It will stop at some point. My mom had her ears pierced and the same thing happened for a few years before her body accepted the jewelry."

"Hmm...I don't want you to go through that but certain piercings are required for you to have as my wife. My position in the church is important. In order to do my job to the best of my ability, my wife has to accept and follow the laws set before her by me, like I have to accept, follow, and enforce the laws set by our church. Your piercings are a constant reminder that you're mine to protect, honor, and cherish."

"I accepted the laws here the minute I met you. I want to follow your laws and your commands. I trust you." *But do you trust me? Do you believe me?*

He smiled and placed his hand on her thigh. "I know... but accepting the laws and doing everything under your control to follow them are two different things." He sighed and softened his tone.

"I will follow the laws, Logan," she said. "I have a natural inclination to do the right thing, and the only reason I was held up at the boutique was because Riley stood in my way from following you, and she grabbed me.

I want to be with you, always. There will be times when I'm not physically able to follow your order, but it won't be cause for punishment. I will never disobey you or intentionally ignore a community or church law. I hope you know that." She patted her chest over her heart. "I hope that you feel my honesty in your heart."

He placed his hand over hers, stopping her from moving her hand. "I do feel it. Part of the truth I feel in your spirit that is one with mine is that you're part of God's plan for this community. You were placed here to marry me and to increase the balance of good in this world. Your heart and spirit...your words, your deeds are as pure as God's healing love. The jewelry and piercings also indicate, to those who know, that you're married to the Enforcer of the Law within the national church body. My position is only held by an angel or a cluster of angels. I am also a National Elder in the church, which can be held by men or women who have gone through a series of spiritual testing to ensure their soul is void of unadulterated evil. Do you understand what that means?"

You're an angel like my mom. "You're part of an anonymous team of men and women—and *angels*—who fight to rid evil from infiltrating the community, church, and a majority of the countries in the world."

"Yes. That's right. Since my position deals with the law, you have to follow each and every rule, as do I. If you break a rule, you will be punished by me. If I break a rule, I am punished by God as the rest of the national elder board watch. I have broken rules and been punished. It's not a pleasant experience. No one is perfect, so you will make mistakes, like I will. We must keep each other accountable to minimize any errors." He turned down the gravel road to his home.

"I'll do my best, but what kind of rules would I break?"

"Interfering in an exorcism I'm conducting. You might disagree with the punishments I dole out or want to allow someone to enter our town that I expressly forbid entrance. I am responsible for every single person who lives in Exorcise, Texas. If someone dies prematurely, it is my fault. There are no drugs, no theft, no murders, no crime whatsoever because I perform my duties all the time. I have no days off, unless I receive God's permission and then specifically ask my grandfather to step in and perform my duties. There are many rules that would be easy for either of us to break. Your instinct is to heal others, so you might want to heal someone without first consulting God and then asking the person for permission."

"You must constantly be praying, even when you're talking," she said. The gravity of his position in the city, the community, the church, and nationally began to sink in.

"I pray and am vigilant. God has gifted me with abilities that transcend this world. He's, also, given you other-worldly abilities that you've yet to discover." He parked the truck inside the garage on the side of the house. "Now tell me what you know about your body's healing properties. Do you have to use your blood to heal people? Can you heal by touch? How long have you been actively healing?"

Aurora's hands tingled with energy. "I've been healing minor injuries ever since I can remember, but when I heal,

I take on that person's pain. Although with spirit cleansings, pain isn't involved at all. But the cleansings are temporary most of the time. I don't know everything I can do. My mother said that she'd explain the kinds of gifts that I have and how to use them, only she didn't...and now she's gone. I'll never know all of my healing abilities."

"There's something else you haven't told me." He took her hand in his. "I don't want to force it out of you. Please, just talk to me. Your secrets are safe with me."

"My mother said that I was different than her. She healed bodies and occasionally was able to heal a person's spirit as long as I was in the room. But she said I inherited gifts from my father that kept me from taking on any darkness. But my dad didn't have any supernatural gifts. He wasn't an angel. He struggled to choose goodness over evil, failing each test he was faced with temptation. Mom loved him so much, but her light faded with each passing year. Her once bright white light which surrounded her and everyone around her turned into a murky and sticky light gray with ribbons of a thorny darkness cutting and constricting the layers of white and turning them darker and darker whenever she went somewhere alone with my dad. Dad pushed her to do things that compromised her soul. What kind of gift could he have given me?"

He nodded, seemingly processing her words. "This might be hard to hear, but it is the truth. You are a full-fledged angel. Only an angel, not a half-breed, could be my perfect match. Only an angel with healing abilities would be my perfect match. You had two types of healing angels as your parents. The man you called your dad isn't biologically related to you. I'm not sure who your father is, but I know who to ask."

"My dad *is* my father. I have his smile," she said. "And Dad never would've married Mom, if I wasn't his."

But that would explain the distance he kept from me. He rarely hugged me. Never kissed my forehead. The older I got the less time he spent with me. Mom hid my abilities from him for years. She made all the decisions for me, shielded me from his darkness as much as she could. He never told me that he loved me. Maybe he knew I wasn't his.

He tipped his head as if he was listening to someone talk. "You have healing qualities in your touch. You're afraid of the power you possess...a power your mother had...a power your dad abused for his own...Oh, Lord, no." He opened his palm and raised his hand in the air. "He told people about you. He brought evil directly to—"

He quickly made a fist and swiped it down against the seat. He opened the car door and swung his hand out, opening his palm like he was throwing a live grenade into the yard. He stepped out of the truck and stared at the opening of the garage.

A painful sense of guilt and curiosity filled her heart. *How do you know all that? Who are you listening to? Why can't I hear what you hear? What were you doing with your hand? What are the rest of your gifts?*

She exited the truck out of the driver's side and stood behind him. "All of that is true. My father told some people about my mother. He told them about me, but I don't think they believed that I was like my mother. She had green eyes with specs of gold like my grandmother had. Mine are blue like every man on my grandmother's side of the family. They only turn gold when—"

"They turn gold when you're in the process of healing a wound, either yours or someone else's. Your dad is *not* your biological father. He can't be. But who is your biological father?"

"My dad *is* my biological father." *He has to be. Mom would never choose to be with him, to be with a man who gravitated to evil unless he was my father. She wouldn't choose him over an angel who helped make me.*

"No. He's not. Your mother had angel blood in her veins, and your biological father would have had angel blood, too. The guy I grew up with who told me he was your father had basic human blood inside him. There was nothing special in his DNA. He had no special abilities. He came from the darker side of humanity and his family was sent here to cleanse their line. This town was named for what we do—exorcise evil from humans. I exorcise evil, as my father and mother had done before me, and my grandfather continues to do when he hears the calling. The man who raised you was born *human*. You are born from two full-blooded angels, like me, or there wouldn't have been a one hundred percent match between us. I should've known immediately that you were an angel. I wondered if you were, but you hide your true self well. And God shielded that knowledge from me to test my faith." He frowned.

"I'm a half-breed. That's what my mother said. My father, in all his failings, is my biological father. I can heal and cleanse my own body and spirit, and sometimes, I can do it for others, too. I've inherited that ability from my mother. I think that she was part-angel, not untainted like you. You're...so pure and strong and handsome. You're amazing."

The frustration he'd been consumed with seemed to vanish with her confession of love.

His voice softened even more, and a gentle smile donned his lips. "For you to cleanse a person's spirit, Aurora, you must have more than one parent whose lineage came from the fallen angels here on earth. And there are specific angels who cleanse and heal. Your father had no such lineage. You come from two separate angel bloodlines who heal. Your form is human, but when God calls on you, your form will shift and enhance. Your spirit will expand and your true identity as one of God's chosen angels will rise. You're an angel with jobs to perform. I come from two different types of angel bloodlines both of whom uphold the law and carry out justice. I never expected to have a perfect match walk into my town, let alone come to live in my home."

She curled her arms around his narrow waist, hoping he'd turn around. "I *was* matched with another man in the church, so maybe I'm who I think I am—a half-breed angel with limited healing abilities."

"Aurora, I found out this morning that you were matched with my biological grandfather. He is an angel who walks this earth and has for thousands of years. He isn't interested in having a young woman as his wife, and his heart is still broken over losing my grandmother." He covered her hands with his and guided them downward over his bulge. "As soon as he sees you, he's going to wish he hadn't declined the match."

"I would've chosen you. I wanted you from the first moment I saw you," she admitted. "But I don't think I'm like you the way you think I am. My father *is* my biological father. My mother loved him, and he loved her."

He turned around and his eye color morphed from blue to swirls of silver and gold. "For a baby to be born with angel qualities passed down, both parents would have those qualities—Meaning both parents would either be angels, or one angel and one human with at least eighty-percent angel genetics. There are few humans who are compatible to procreate with an angel. The human must be special and anointed by God as such. Their spirits must be pure. I only know of one living-human who fits that special circumstance. Most humans join in partnerships with demons, not angels..." He continued telling her about the types of demons who mate with humans.

Chaotic thoughts whirled in her head as he inundated her with what seemed like nonsense but she knew from experience was the truth. She had run across many demons over the years. Fighting them was impossible, especially with her father inviting them home. "Why would my mother leave this town with my dad, unless he was my biological father?"

"I don't know, but an angel's spirit was scattered across this land not long after you were conceived."

"What do you mean that the angel's spirit was scattered?" *Do you mean an angel died? My mother's body burned to nothing but ash, and her spirit...I felt her spirit shatter. The energy released from her death knocked the wind out of me. My knees buckled. I fell to my hands and knees. I wasn't even with her and I felt the shockwave of her death down deep into the marrow of my bones.*

"When an angel with a spirit of light dies," he said. "Their spirit scatters across the land they call home. Pieces of their spirit rushes to those they love before that spirit comes back together and flies up to Heaven to be with God, once again. If the angel's spirit is tainted, the angel can be blocked from Heaven and dragged down to Hell—or more often than not, the angel willingly follows a demon or a human who sold their soul to the devil—joining the forces of darkness. When this happens, the physical body combusts, leaving a dark stain and flakes of oily black ash."

"Can they be in Hell, but still fight for God? For the good of the world?" *Mom would fight for me. She would never intentionally hurt me. She'd protect me, even in the afterlife. She loved me.*

He gazed at her, cupping her cheeks. "We choose sides when we live in this earthly realm. There is no middle ground once our physical body dies. The mother you knew is gone. If you see her again, she will attempt to deceive you. You must remember the first two rules of the church. Pray to God and obey me. My orders should always align with what God tells you to do." He gently pressed his forehead to hers. "I'm so sorry."

While she tried to keep her emotions under control, her chin quivered. Tears filled her eyes. "My mom wouldn't hurt me. She'd join me in helping people, even in the afterlife."

"She's no longer your mother, Aurora. Her spirit stands with Lucifer and his demons, not with God and us. I saw the photos of the crime scene. Now that I know what she was, what you are." He closed his eyes. "I believe your father was killed in battle soon after you were conceived. If my parents and grandfather knew your mother was an angel, they could've helped her. If they'd known about her pregnancy..." He shook his head and inhaled, opening his eyes. "I'll find out who your biological father is and his abilities."

"I don't want you to be disappointed when you find out I'm not that special."

"You are *that* special." He made a rumbling noise and ran his fingers through her hair to the back of her head, holding her gently. "You have to be completely honest with me."

"I promise, I'll be honest with you all the time." *I love you.*

While one of his hands caressed down her neck, over her breast and down her side, he glanced at her chest. "Do you want to make love to me?"

"Wait, what?" *That is NOT what I expected.* Her gaze drifted down his delicious body, noticing Logan's hand rubbing his bulge. Whatever he saw or heard or sensed changed his focus.

"I want you. Do you want me?" he asked.

She closed her eyes. "I do. But I'm worried about the church and making sure we have everything we need to stay within the rules. I don't want to get in trouble." She gazed up at him and was lost in the hypnotic silver and gold in his eyes. "I'm also concerned about the church knowing about my healing capabilities."

"Why?" He nuzzled under her ear and kissed along her neck.

She slipped her hands under his T-shirt, searching for the spark that ignites the deep connection between them. "We can't have a church where no one ever gets sick, where people get addicted to the rush of energy and vitality and seek it out—from me. The good that comes out of healing a person turns bad almost instantly. It's a new road to addiction for most people."

"For humans like your father?" he asked, halting his kisses for a fraction of a minute.

She nodded. "He tried to stop, but he couldn't. It wasn't that he didn't love us. The high of healing usually changes the person who just wants the adrenaline rush of feeling incredible, without any compassion to the pain it inflicts on the healer."

"Your mother was a medical tech," he said. "Did she heal people while at work?"

"Sometimes, she did, but it was rare. She told me that she'd hear what she believed was God's voice and only then follow the call to heal. She said that patients would recall an angel coming to them on their death bed. But it was my mom who gave them a small infusion of her blood, not the angelic figure they proclaimed healed them." She pressed her palm over his heart, under his shirt. While she felt the thumping of his heart beating, she scooted closer to him. *I should tell you that I love you. I think I'm the one addicted to you.*

"The patients saw her true form, her spiritual form," he said. "I hear God's word whispering to me. Like you, I see the light of the spirit that surrounds people. But instead of searching for sickness to heal, I search for justice to absolve or punish. I find deceit within a person's spirit and force the truth to shine through within confession. The dark root of the lie is unearthed, and if the person refuses to admit their wrongdoing, such evil forms from that falsehood that pain moves from the soul of the person to their physical being. Bones break, organs shut down, and death eventually takes control, burning their bodies to ash, crushing their spirit until only a smattering of cosmic dust remains, if they continue to refuse the exorcism. You haven't even touched the surface of your powers, whereas I've mastered the nuances of mine."

His chest expanded as he inhaled and a pure white light burst outward, surrounding him.

She blinked as his spirit drew her closer, and the desire to make love to him brought heat throughout her body. Juices lubricated her sex for him. She wanted him to carry her inside and make love to her. Heck, she'd take off her jeans in three seconds flat and ride him right here, right now. But instead of going with the flow of her desire, she opened her mouth to say what her heart believed. "I'm not like you."

"You are," he mumbled.

Tired of an argument she couldn't win, she asked about his family. "What happened to your parents?" she asked.

"Both my parents and my grandmother passed away battling demons. The three were Law Angels like me and my grandfather. They'd lived thousands of years. Their deaths were horrific, seeing their spirits scattered...to see their lights snuffed out by demons before my grandfather and I could save them was..."

She wanted to comfort him, but he seemed lost in the memories.

"As soon as we arrived at the battle, we released the power of God—judgment rained down on the demons and the humans who'd given Lucifer's army shelter to tear down our city, our church, and kill angels."

"Are you...are *we* in danger?".

"No, I'm stronger than my parents ever were, even

when they were together. My grandfather is here to protect and stand by us, too, and his strength is more like mine. There are others here who God has shined his light on. They will rise up and stand next to us, if a horde of demons come this way. I'm here for a reason. I'm here to keep this land and these people safe from evil. To cleanse the community from their addictions. To exorcise demons from their bodies. To crush the darkness and release the light shining within each human living within my territory. If evil has taken root and been fully accepted by the person's spirit, they will refuse the cleansing and leave our town, or face death."

"A man killed my parents. No demons were present." She averted her gaze at the small lie, while the scene of the murders flooded her consciousness. *Knife cuts so deep… blood everywhere…a haze of dark energy clinging to the bodies, to the walls, to the weapons, to the rug where Mom's body was burned, leaving nothing of her but a smattering of slick, oily ash.*

"The man had to have a demon dwelling inside him. From what I've heard, read, and you've told me, the murderer brought friends—demonic friends. They leave trails of their true beings—sluggish black fog that resembles black tar which clings to whatever they've touched."

"Everybody around my dad left spiritual markings. Tar-like substances were smeared on the walls and doorknobs, stairs…*everywhere*. My father held the darkness inside him, but that doesn't mean he was a demon. And my mother should have lived. She healed instantly, like I do. She bled and her heart was broken as a teen, like any normal person…"

She hated that tears slid down her cheeks, but she couldn't stop them. He hadn't experienced much of her emotional outbursts, but the more she talked about the murders of her mother and father, the more powerful each honest emotion became, forcing them to the surface. She ached to feel her mom's arms around her, comforting her. She'd give anything to hear her mom's sweet voice telling her that as long as they were together, they'd always be okay. "I miss her."

He sighed and pulled her against his chest, embracing her in a comforting hug. "I'm sorry. I'm not much of a nurturer but I want to be…for you. I want to be your place of shelter, the one you run to for conversation, or help, or for any reason whatsoever."

"You are all those things. But I need help. I don't know how to fight. I heal people. I don't hurt them, but they want to hurt me. *Riley* wanted to hurt me." She hadn't meant to tell him about Riley, but he needed to know the truth.

"I need to find out more about your biological father in order to teach you the correct techniques to protect yourself from situations like you were in with Riley."

"Logan, I love you. I wanted to marry you the minute I arrived. I wanted to be matched with you. I was so happy when my blindfold was taken off and I saw your face." The words she hadn't wanted to say spilled from her mouth as her emotions ran rampant inside her. "I'm sorry I wasn't who you wanted, but I'll do anything to—"

"I wanted you from the second you arrived on my ranch, Aurora. I wanted to make love to you and make you mine. Your parents entrusted you to me as a guardian, but I didn't want to be that to you. I wanted more. I pulled you close every chance I got. I held you in my arms longer than I should have. I fantasized of you beneath me. I wanted the woman who was my perfect match to be you. When my blindfold was taken off, I hadn't expected it to be you. Guilt filled me, because of who I am, of my position in the church, of the strict life you'll be forced to live forever. I was born into this life. It comes naturally to me. You didn't choose my life. You ended up with it…Aurora, you don't even believe you were born from two angels." He sighed.

"I would have chosen your life had I been given a choice. I love your rules. I love that you expect my obedience." She pulled his T-shirt up over his head, and the heated desire that constantly boiled under the surface all the time flowed to the surface. *I need you to make love to me, to comfort me, to be my husband, not a detective picking apart my lineage and childhood. I need you to protect my heart, not crush it.*

"You're intoxicating," he mumbled. "I feel you inside me as if we were one person." He stepped backward, grabbing his T-shirt as her arms slid out from around him. "I need you to tell me the secret you're hiding. I promise that I will not abuse your gift or utter your secret to anyone who doesn't need to know." He rolled up his shirt and shoved it in his back pocket, leaving half of it out, hanging down over her ass and thigh.

She held out her hand, palm up. "I will tell you, but it will put you in danger as well as me and possibly this community."

He clasped his hand over hers. "No one will harm you. God has given me authority over this community, these people, and this land. No one can stand against God. Thousands, even trillions could come and surround our borders, and they would perish. But we would not perish, for we have God's promise to prosper us and protect us because we turn to Him for all things. He is our friend and He loves us. He's set this land apart as His, and we are His people because we believe in Him."

"My grandmother was born a pure-blooded Lockhart angel," she confessed. "Her father told the leader of the Lockhart family that she had died in childbirth, but in reality, he'd stolen her away to a friend who raised her. The Lockharts kill their females. My grandmother had one child, my mother. I don't know my biological grandfather. He wasn't in our lives, and Grandmother never spoke of him. But she married a nice man who protected her secret and brought her here to Exorcise, Texas, where she raised my mother. My mother fell in love with my father, leaving here. When I was born, I was different than my mother and grandmother. I had inherited the ice-blue eyes of the Lockhart bloodline. Grandmother told my mom and dad that we could never come back, not even to visit her, or I would be recognized and killed somewhere along the way. That they'd found her and she was on the run, too."

"Do you know when your grandmother died?" he asked.

"Not long after I was born. She was on her way to Las Vegas to talk to someone. Mom told me that my dad was born from the Vogel bloodline, but to never tell or the peace between the Lockharts and the Vogels would dissolve into a war unlike any the world has seen in many thousands of years. Dad was a Vogel and even he didn't know it. I don't know how true any of that is. Mom told me that angels couldn't die, but they can. She did. She lied to me, something I didn't think she had the capability to do."

Logan looked up at the sky. "The man who you considered your dad wasn't a Vogel. Your mother was talking about your biological father. But Vogels aren't healing angels, they're warrior angels. They possess the power to heal themselves instantly. In order to heal someone else, the Vogel men and women must be passionately in love with them. Your father couldn't heal himself, let alone anyone else."

"No. My mom said that my father was from the Vogel line. The Vogels aren't angels. They're addicts and partiers like my dad…like my dad had been. Dad never talked about his family. Mom always told me never to speak a word of the truth to Dad or he'd get angry, because they disowned him."

He lowered his gaze and stared into her eyes, seemingly searching through her soul. "Your father wasn't a Vogel. Your mother lied to you about your conception. The Vogels would welcome him and you. Their leader is Wenzel Vogel. I've known him for a long time. He's a good man, although he's unpredictable. Some call him unstable. He's passionate and strategic, not unstable. He's old, very old. He's older than my grandfather, but he perpetually looks like he's in his mid-twenties." He closed his eyes and swallowed.

"What is wrong?"

"You can heal anyone. I have a friend. He's sick. Really sick. He's a member of our church and knows I'm an angel. He'll know you're not like everyone else. He sees and hears God's voice, like I do. While in my presence, he was anointed by God. I stood with my grandfather as the man's spirit went through an awakening. A cloud of fire descended from the heavens and surrounded him. The power was so intense I dropped down to the ground, stretched out in a prostrate position, unable to raise my head. I heard God's voice claiming him—Rager Smithson—as His warrior, as His friend, as His Anointed One."

He gazed at her with silver and gold swirling within his irises. "When I arose, my friend's eyes glowed with gold. His aura was pure gold. His pale skin was speckled with gold where it had been torn. He hadn't been fully healed from his sicknesses, but his spirit was healed. His life force was strong. His mind was sharp. When he's on a mission from God, he's like an angel with the force of God's strength in his sword. He defeats all who stand in his way. No one survives."

"Why would he care about me and what I can do?" she asked.

"Because he's in love, and he's healed her from an evil device a demon had attached to her bones and organs in an attempt to kill her—because she is a Lockhart and survived the ritual when all other females of their clan had not. I believe she is closely related to you, possibly a cousin. I believe you might be able to heal my friend, or possibly heal several women in our church and sister churches with your abilities, but I'm not sure."

"My touch is addictive."

"Yes. It can be, but I'm with you. You're safe with me.

"You don't know that." *Unless God sends me some kind of sign in contradiction to what I've seen growing up, it's not safe for me to heal without safeguards in place, and I don't know what those safeguards are.*

"I do." He swept her up into his arms. He strode forward, tossing off her boots to the right of the door to the house and pulling off his own. While she pressed the button to close the garage, he opened the door and stepped over the threshold. He kicked the door closed, passed through the kitchen and moved straight to his bedroom. Once inside, he plopped her on the bed and stripped her naked.

"Logan, what are you doing?" A deep desire to make love to him surged through her.

Electricity crackled in the air between them.

"I'm about to show you a small portion of my angel form." He unzipped his jeans, letting out his hard cock. "You're going to love it." He pushed down his jeans and underwear, tossing them along with his shirt hanging from the back of his jeans on the floor near the door to the closet. His cock bobbed against his abs as he strode to her.

You're the most gorgeous man I've ever seen. Juices flooded her pussy. The need for his cock pumping inside her, filling her with his seed, became overwhelming. She spread her legs and he crawled between them.

Her thoughts twirled like a tornado with what pleasures he might give her. He wanted a baby to grow inside her and she wanted one, too. Her body heated to a fiery desire for him to dominate her, to make love to her, to... taste her blood. She wanted to heal him from any thoughts of his moments with Riley.

Juices drenched her pussy, begging for him to enter. "I need you right now."

He moaned and tipped his head back as she arched her chest, pushing her tits up toward his face. Her nipples beaded. Droplets of golden fluid trickled down from the piercing holes. The crosses on the rings jingled and fell down against the undercurve of her breasts.

He dropped down into a pushup. With his hands at

her shoulders and his cock pressing against her juicy entrance, he gazed into her eyes. "I love you."

He thrust.

She countered his thrust with her own. Her breasts jiggled, jingling the rings. She wanted to burn all memories of Riley from Logan's mind. She wanted him to forget that he'd ever dated Riley. That he'd touched her. She wanted him to forget the sound of Riley's voice. She wanted his child growing inside her, cementing their bond, their marriage, their commitment, eliminating any hold Riley had over him.

His thrusts came faster and deeper, insistent.

She arched her back as far as physically possible, needing to feel as much of his skin against hers.

An electrical surge rocked her body. Her pussy creamed as her uterus contracted. She grabbed hold of his shoulders and rolled her body against his hard muscles. "More, Logan. More."

His lips suctioned tightly to the flesh of her neck, then he nibbled over the spot.

She caressed over his shoulders and wrapped her legs around his.

He curled his arm around her back, his hand spanning from hip-to-hip along the lower curve of her spine. While he thrust and ground his pelvis, driving his cock into her, the energy in the room sizzled.

She gasped as the world slowed its rotation and a golden light exploded around him.

He raised his head and the blue of his eyes shined with specks of silver and gold. His creamy, porcelain skin now shimmered with gold, giving him the illusion of a deep suntan.

The softest and most beautiful cocoon of downy-white feathers encircled them.

"You have wings?" she whispered.

"Yes." He grunted. "Need you. I need you."

She used every muscle in her body to push down as he thrust up. They rose and fell, skin gliding against skin, chasing bliss.

He pounded one glorious spot after another. "Come with me."

With that one command, her belly clenched. Her pussy clamped down on his girth. She writhed beneath him, screaming his name.

Heat flooded into her sex.

He shuddered and stilled. "I love you, Aurora. I love you more than you'll ever know."

She softened beneath him. "I can't wait to make a family with you."

Logan rolled to his side, taking her with him, joined together, facing each other. He suddenly shut off his emotions as his cock slid from her pussy. "We'll talk more later. Go get cleaned up and dressed for chores."

Wham. Bam. Thank you, ma'am. Time for chores. She rolled over and grabbed a new pair of jeans and a pink T-shirt from the dresser and hurried into the bathroom. She braced her hands against the sink and looked into the mirror. Her skin was flushed a pretty pink. Her nipples were red and the gold crosses on the rings swayed softly from the slight movement of her breasts. The curves of her body had expanded a little, not that anyone but she would notice. Seeing that small change made her think about her parents. She looked for that smile her mother always said reminded her of her father.

But the smile looking back at her didn't have her father's thin lips or his extra-wide mouth. Her smile had full lips, a bow in the top, a...*There's no resemblance to my father. He wasn't my dad. I was just part of the package. Mom lied. Who is my father?*

The adjoining door to the bathroom opened.

"Sorry," Riley said. "I'll..." Her gaze met Aurora's. "Everything okay?"

Aurora covered her breasts and nodded. "Just..." She exhaled, still catching her breath. *I'm naked. I've got Logan's seed on the inside of my thighs. What are you doing here?*

"I'm sorry about earlier. You're exactly what he needs, and it seems he's exactly what you need," Riley said. "I've heard about perfect matches, but I've never actually seen one until now."

The door to the bedroom opened and Logan stood wearing his jeans low on his hips. "What's going on in here?"

"I walked in on Aurora. I wasn't thinking," Riley said. "I should've knocked. And I'm leaving now." She pivoted and walked out, closing the door behind her. "Again, I'm sorry."

"It's okay," Aurora said, loudly. *Maybe seeing me naked with a sex glow will end your chase for my husband.*

Logan grabbed a washcloth and turned on the hot water at the sink faucet. "Did she upset you?"

"No, sir. I'm just taking a minute to regroup."

"Are you sore between your legs?"

"Not at all. Remember, I'm an instant healer." *I'm a little embarrassed that Riley saw me like this.* "I feel pretty incredible."

"Me, too. My entire body is buzzing with energy." He

wet the washcloth and rinsed it out. "We need a honeymoon. I need a week of uninterrupted time with you."

Knock. Knock.

"What?" Logan grumbled.

"Sorry," Riley shouted. "I need y'all to make a few decisions out here."

He growled, whispering in her ear, "I was going to take you back to bed." He kissed her cheek. "I'll go make a decision on whatever needs to be decided. Hurry up. We're going to set a timer to see how long it takes us to finish chores." He opened the door and Riley peeked in.

"Is she okay?" Riley asked. "She looks rattled."

"She's fine." He closed the door. "What do I need to look at?"

"You're moody. You're never moody. What's with you?" Riley said.

"I want to spend time alone with my wife. I don't want to do this. I don't want people over. I don't want to do anything but make love to my wife."

"Woah," Riley said. "Slow down. You're going to have to give the girl a little break between sessions or you'll hurt her."

"I won't hurt her. I know what she can and can't handle. You need to stay out of it."

"Fine. I'll organize a group to do your chores for the next few weeks. Food is on the way…"

By the hard tones coming from the other side of the door, Logan seemed to argue about something with Riley, but the hushed voices prevented Aurora from eavesdropping.

Another door closed, shutting out all noise but Aurora's own breathing.

She gazed at the mirror once more. The pink in her face was still there. The longer she stared into the mirror, the more she could see the changes in her eyes, making them golden like her mother's after she'd used her gift.

The gold outlining Aurora's pupils expanded and filled in the variances of color in her blue irises.

Within seconds, her eye color had completely morphed to gold, leaving only the slightest remnants of the original ice-blue. She now carried the mark of her female ancestors, the golden eyes of a healer, the sign of the power that flowed within her spirit—the power of youth and strength and unparalleled health. A power she'd most likely gifted to Logan, too, although she wasn't sure it could truly be given to others, not permanently. The truth is that she didn't know enough about the powers her mother had told her about, or if she had more powers than only those.

CHAPTER FIFTEEN

Logan

When Riley confessed to peeking in on Logan and Aurora making love, he stormed out of his house before he could exact revenge. He'd felt her presence and cut off the cuddling that always came after sex. He probably caused Aurora some heartache or insecurity. His wife was sensitive and empathic and carried too many burdens for one person. Had he known that his friendship with Riley would one day interfere in his marriage, he never would have been intimate with her. That was his mistake to rectify.

As for Riley, he'd have to do something about her behavior. She'd already confessed to bringing decorations and furniture into the house that might remind him of her, not for helping Aurora make her own claim on the house.

"I'm sorry," Riley shouted. "I'm jealous. You love her. You never loved me like that."

"I *never* loved you," he yelled. "I *liked* you."

"Why *her*?" Riley ran after him. "Why not me?"

"You and I fight," he shouted. "You're perfect for someone who needs to be challenged in their personal life. I don't. I'm constantly battling something or someone. I need peace in my life, not more struggle. You never understood that. It's not who you are. We're not the same in any way, Riley. We're not alike at all."

He turned on his boot heel and strode around the house, along the road leading to the barn. The house looked great inside, but it did remind him of Riley, not his Aurora. Part of him wanted to throw all the stuff out of his house and burn it in front of Riley, but that would send him down a path he would never go. He made a vow to uphold the law, under all circumstances, not destroy it or destroy a person's spirit because they angered him.

"Logan, stop and talk to me," Riley shouted.

He turned around and took a deep breath, centering his power and concentrating on the peace that came with his position in God's hierarchy. "Riley, you need to get the stuff you brought over and take it all back. Every little thing that Aurora didn't pick out. My house is not a battle zone. You're not going to wreak havoc in my marriage because you wanted something that didn't and wasn't ever going to happen."

"I wouldn't try to ruin your marriage, not on purpose." So many colors swirled in her aura and drifted off as she stood staring at him.

"You tried to bring chaos into my marriage, Riley. You tried, and that's the truth. Here's some more truth for you. My wife's parents were murdered. We're leaving for Atlanta in a few days where she will have to face her parents' murderer. There is a high likelihood that she will also have to see that man walk out, unscathed." *And there is nothing I can do about it.* He clenched his fists. "The world doesn't revolve around you, Riley. It never has, and it never will. Grow up. Grow up and get any of your jealousy-tainted home goods out of my house. Aurora needs a place that has her imprint, not yours."

Her head snapped back like he'd hit her. "I'll ask Aurora what she wants."

"No. Don't ask Aurora anything. Take everything from your boutique back. We'll buy from somewhere else."

"You didn't tell me her parents were..." Riley lowered her gaze. "That's why she came here. She had nowhere else to go?"

"Stop arguing with me. Do as I say," he ordered.

"I'm not arguing. I'm asking." She huffed and shoved her hands in the back pockets of her tight jeans.

"Your intentions say otherwise," he said.

"She came here because her father trusted you to take care of her," she continued talking. "I wonder how he would feel about you taking his little girl to your bed." She poked at his weaknesses, one of her many talents. "Deflowering his little princess in the church *he hated.* Good one, Logan."

"Both her parents trusted me, and they were smart to do so." He stepped closer to her and made a wide circle with his hand front of her, calling forth her spirit for cleansing. *You call out for evil whenever you don't get your way. You need to start calling out to God.* "You keep saying you're sorry, and then you incite anger and hostility. Are you truly sorry?"

Riley trembled as the darkness in her spirit crept along the outskirts, building strength for an attack at the heart of her soul. She was a prime target for a demon takeover. Her grandparents on both sides, her parents, and siblings all succumbed to demons. The allure of riches and fame sucked them in, allowing an opening for evil. It's a miracle that Riley survived childhood in a house of demons, let alone chose to come here, begging for an exorcism. She'd come a long way in the last five years, but she had triggers that ran deep. Between medication, therapy, and his constant watch, her pure spirit had strengthened and she was flourishing at work and in the community. But he should've known his marriage to Aurora would endanger her.

"What's happening?" she whined.

Furious with himself, and his lack of foresight, he stood still, watching for her aura to shake off the evil. At least now, she acknowledged the shift in her spirit. This showed progress. *She* showed progress.

"You're being attacked, Riley," he said. "Close your eyes and take inventory of your body and spirit. Feel for my intervention." He shifted his hands, forcing the center core of her aura, the whitest and most powerful layer, to expand. "Do you feel me?"

"Yes." She moaned. "You feel so good."

"Have you been taking your medicine? Talking to your therapist?"

She rushed toward him.

He sighed and opened his arms in time for her embrace. "You haven't been following your protocol, have you?" He knew the answer. He could see and feel it in her spirit. But as soon as she wrapped her arms around him, the evil crumbled in on itself and vanished.

While she breathed against him, anger rose once again.

"I'm sorry. I'm trying. I'm really trying. I looked at my list of things to do, and I even went over what to do when I was feeling out of control." She sobbed in his arms. "I didn't take the steps. I ignored them. I don't like that feeling, but it's so familiar that it's almost comforting."

He cradled her head and brought it to his chest like he'd been doing since she came to Exorcise, Texas. "It's a destructive type of comfort, Riley. It weighs you down, not lifts you up."

She sagged against him, reminding him so much of the first time he met her. She'd been in bad shape, but she had two choices when she finished her jail sentence. The first was to go back to her life where a gang death awaited her. The second was to get on a bus to the closed community of Exorcise and start fresh, with new rules, new people, and a new career. She chose the latter. When she arrived, she was the only one left on the bus. The only one who didn't exit the bus on the many stops along the road. She was like so many others in the community who came here because it was a life or death decision.

But there was always something special about Riley. The woman was fierce, but that first day, she'd given every ounce of fight to get to town. She didn't have any more fight in her. She needed someone else to fight for her, and he did. He pulled her into his arms and exorcised the demons clawing to get inside her soul. He had carried her into the church and helped prepare a place for her in the community. Those first few years were hard. He'd visited her every day, checking on her soul's health, her mind's health, and her body's health.

"What are you so angry about, Riley?"

"I want a perfect match from our church," she sniffled. "I want someone to love me, instantly. I want what you have with Aurora. I want that. And I want you. I love you."

"I love you, too—" He turned his head at the heart-breaking gasp behind him.

Aurora trembled where she stood on the porch.

"It's not what you think," he shouted. He couldn't leave Riley when she was so vulnerable, or she could backslide again. She'd done it before. He had to get her to her therapist and doctor before he released her from his care. This was one of the many parts of his job that Aurora would have to accept. "Riley needs help and I—"

"It's fine," Aurora cut him off. "I'll finish the chores." She pivoted, turning her back to him, but her bright white aura remained white, showing no signs of distress. Yet, he knew in his heart that he had hurt her.

He'd have to talk to his grandfather about her strange behavior. Healing angels wore their heart on their sleeve, not hidden in a secret place he couldn't find. The Lockhart family of Healing Angels didn't have the capability to hide anything from him, not even their precious secrets locked inside boxes in their vaults all over the world.

"She's upset," Riley whispered.

"Yes, she is." *What kind of special angel combination is my wife?* "Let's get you to the church, where you can heal." *Until I can decipher Aurora's ancestry, I'll have to keep an extra set of eyes on her.*

CHAPTER SIXTEEN

Aurora

He loves her. He LOVES her. My husband loves another woman.

Aurora stumbled toward the couch in the living room. "The leather couch looks great in this space. It looks like *Riley* married him. Everything looks like *her*. The new pillows, throws, couches, chairs all look like she lives here with him. Nothing looks like me."

She plopped down on the most comfortable couch she'd ever sat on. "I don't even know what would look like me. I've never owned anything."

She picked up a dark brown fur floor pillow and held it against her chest. "The woman has great taste." She slouched and dropped her head back against the couch. *Logan wanted her but got stuck with me. What am I going to do?*

While she pondered her choices, which amounted to none, a white light rolled into the room like a morning fog covering the soccer field at her old high school. The light shifted from white to gold to blue to crimson and then white again as a wave engulfed her in a loving embrace.

"Aurora?" a man called out. "Are you decent in there, young lady?"

On instinct, she stood up, tossed the pillow on the floor and looked for a way out.

A man who looked like Logan walked toward her. He unbuttoned his navy jacket and sat on the new cream leather couch that Riley had delivered today. "I'm Daniel Hutchison, Logan's grandfather." He ran his hands through his brown hair that had touches of silver on the sides. The man didn't look old enough to be anyone's grandfather. He didn't have a single wrinkle on his face.

"It's nice to meet you." *What are you doing here?* "I'm Aurora."

He smiled, showing off straight, white teeth. "Logan is..." He sighed and shrugged. "Riley is a handful, but she's improving every year that she remains in our crime-free city. Enough about Riley and her demons. How can I help you prepare the house? Maybe shop for furniture?" He ran his hand over the seat of the couch. "This is nice, but it isn't you. Don't be afraid to brighten the place up. Logan would have white walls, a bed, and a soaking tub and nothing else, if he could get away with it. And those things are already here."

"I don't know what to buy to make it look like me. I think Logan would prefer Riley's taste in furniture and dishes and everything else that makes a house a home." *He wants her, not me.*

"Logan doesn't prefer Riley's taste in anything. He wants her to succeed and thrive, like he wants all the residents of this town to prosper and find happiness. He loves every single person who lives here." He exhaled. "Sweet Aurora, my grandson's heart beats for you. He loves you with his entire being. You're written on each individual feather in his wings. You're imprinted on his soul. You are the oxygen filling his lungs."

Without realizing she'd moved, she stood in front of him, within touching distance. "Do you really believe that?"

"Yes, Aurora. I do." He patted the seat next to him. "Sit for a moment with me."

She sat beside him, twisting to face him. "What do I do?"

"You and I are going shopping. I'll make sure whatever you want replaces what is already in this house." He stood up and offered her his hand. "Come with me."

She followed his command, taking his hand. A spark at his touch shocked her. While he helped her up, a lovely warmth softened the initial electrical charge.

He tucked her against his side, continuing to hold her hand. "Never worry, sweet Aurora. Logan and I will protect you to our dying breath."

As he led her outside to a white convertible, parked where Logan's truck usually sat, she smelled the scent of lilacs. She inhaled deeply and gazed up at him. *The scent of lilac is coming from you.*

He opened her car door and she easily slid into the car. He bowed and closed the door.

Already, she missed his comforting touch and wanted it again.

The minute he drove forward, he reached for her hand and she happily held it in her lap.

"Where are we going?" she asked.

"We're going to a furniture gallery run by an artist I've known for a long time. You're going to love him. We're going to help you add beautiful layers to the foundation that Logan has built."

"Sounds good to me." *I was a perfect match with you, too. We have chemistry. I hadn't expected that. I hadn't expected you to be so handsome.*

"I look at you, Aurora, and I think that I was a fool not to fight Logan for your hand in marriage. But Logan was already in love with you and you with him. You and he belong together, but I still get to hold your hand and love you from afar." He squeezed her hand. "And I'll get to love on the grandchildren you and Logan will have in the coming years."

Her cheeks flamed with his bold words. She held her tongue, not that she had anything to say. She didn't have anything to say, but she wondered if holding his hand was wrong. That maybe Logan wouldn't like it. But at the same time, he hadn't inappropriately touched her, and she didn't believe that he would cross that line. She would make sure he didn't cross a line that would damage her marriage with Logan.

"I can't wait to help teach your children all our laws and how to enforce them," he said. "It's one of the greatest joys of my life to protect the people in this town and teach our laws to the ones who come here."

The heat in her cheeks remained, but his enthusiasm for the law warmed her heart. Logan had told her something similar. "Did you teach Logan the laws?"

"No. He was born from two law angels." He said that like she'd know what that meant or entailed.

"Did his father teach him the love of the law and all the rules and consequences?"

"Oh…" He glanced at her. "That's right, you weren't taught about our kind. When two law angels have children, they're automatically law angels. They're born with an innate knowledge of God's law, the rules, and the love of all the people they protect. There is nothing we won't do for our people, no matter how vast our territory. My wife and Logan's parents died protecting this town. They're with God now, never allowed to fall down to earth again…that is until the End of Days."

"I'm sorry," she said.

"It's okay. My work here goes on, and I get to spend it with a new granddaughter who is the love of my grandson's life."

Is he? Did I misinterpret Logan's love for Riley?

"What is your favorite color?" he asked.

"Dusty rose and basil green."

He laughed. "Basil green. That is specific."

"Have you planted basil and watched it grow to maturity?"

"I can't say I have," he said.

"Then we're going to have to plant an herb garden, so you see for yourself the beauty of its color."

"Yes, we will," he replied. "I look forward to it."

"Now what is your favorite color?"

"The summer blue of the Texas sky."

He drove slowly, the wind gently lifting her hair from her shoulders as he asked her all sorts of questions about colors and textures and favorite places. The conversation flowed so easily that she'd forgotten about all her insecurities. She focused on his next question, or his hearty laugh, or the slight tilt of his head toward her when she pondered a response. So far, Daniel Hutchison was turning into her first real friend.

CHAPTER SEVENTEEN

Aurora

The day with Daniel was filled driving from one ranch after another, whose owners kept small galleries in their workshops. She'd picked out rugs and sofas, chairs and pillows, glassware, artwork, and more. There was nowhere to put anything in the convertible, so he had everything delivered.

Everyone she met knew Daniel well and told stories of his patience and love. Some of the people he introduced to her were members of the church while others weren't, but Daniel treated everyone the same. She didn't think about whether there were rules against inviting non-church members to Logan's house during the first couple weeks of marriage and invited everyone over to visit. She even talked with Daniel and some of his closer friends about going back to Georgia to prepare and face the man who'd murdered her parents.

While she waited in the car for Daniel to join her, she gazed at all the herbs and produce growing from raised beds and containers on the side of the house where the specialty glassware studio stood. She hoped that Logan liked the unique pieces for the living room and kitchen, but it was the garden the artist had cultivated on his property that drew her full attention. She'd always wanted a big garden with an array of fruits, vegetables, and herbs. The artist was kind enough to walk her through a portion of his garden. She brushed her fingers over the basil and oregano, over the lemons on the trees, along the thyme, the tomatoes, the onions, and so much more, all in raised beds and containers. The plants grew under her fingertips and a buzzing of happiness filled her spirit so full that she wished to stay for a while longer. She wished to sing to them, but she held back. Remaining focused on preparing the house for visitors proved difficult when such a glorious garden desired her presence. Maybe she could have a garden at Logan's. He had plenty of land. Surely, he could allot a portion of his ranch for her to plant a garden of her own.

While she daydreamed about a future garden that Logan would help her build, Daniel slipped into the car and started the engine. The car purred like a satisfied kitten as he drove down the road. The sun had already set, but he continued the leisurely pace he'd kept all day.

"I think we had a very productive day," he said. "You and Logan are now in compliance with all the newlywed laws of the church and community. And I found the perfect gift for you and Logan in the process."

"No, no, no. You've done so much for me, Daniel. Please, don't give us a gift."

"The gift comes with strings attached." He took her hand in his and squeezed.

"What kind of strings?" There was something about him that made her insides feel soft and gooey, like a warm marshmallow.

"You're going to teach me about herbs and how to tend a garden. I've never done anything like that before, and I want to experience it with you."

"I've never tended a garden, only a very small container of herbs. It had to be small enough that I could transport it from one place to another on a moment's notice. But—and this might sound weird—I know I can manage a fairly large garden." She held her right hand to her heart. "I feel it inside me."

"I know you can, and you do, beautiful Aurora," he said. "Your house should be ready by now with all the decorations and home goods put in place that you chose today. Want to go home and see your husband?"

Boy, that was a loaded question. She wasn't sure she wanted to do either. "Do you think Logan is done dealing with Riley?"

"For now? Yes," he said. "But he isn't done dealing with Riley, not without your help healing her. Logan can chase the evil away from her, but it keeps coming back. Something inside her is attacking her. I think she needs a potion, possibly with basil in it. Pray about your garden and how to heal her completely. Listen and compile a list of ingredients. I'll retrieve whatever you need. Then, and only then, will you and Logan be free from her interference. And in her healing, you will free Riley from the constant battle with the evil that is trying to drag her down to Hell and take a piece of you with her."

"I didn't think that could happen here." *Logan said I was safe here.*

"Not on our land, it doesn't," he said. "But if she strays and steps outside the safety of our sacred land, death is a reality she is likely to face. If she loses her battle with evil, she will try and drag you away from Logan and force you outside our borders with her—she will fail to take you, but she will try. Logan and I remain constantly vigilant, especially for those in our community whom we must exorcise one demon after another after another. Riley is one of those people."

"I didn't know," she said. "I think she's dangerous, not just to me, but others."

"You're right. She is. But she doesn't want to be. Next time you see her, touch her hand and allow your natural abilities to take over. Seek out the truth in her heart. Trust Logan to stand as your strength. Trust your natural instincts to heal her. I believe that you and Riley will become friends. Did you know her favorite flower is a white orchid?"

"They're so delicate and beautiful."

"And they need special care," he said. "You can tell a lot about a person by their favorite flower." He turned down Logan's drive and parked behind Logan's truck. He faced her. "Thank you for spending the day with me. I'll be looking after the ranch while you're in Georgia." He raised her hand to his lips and kissed her knuckles. "Logan and I enjoy chocolate and caramel; in case you were wondering."

While she laughed, he released her hand.

"Off you go, before I steal you away," he teased.

She stepped out of the car and closed the door. She stood and waved as he drove away.

With the night lights leading the way to the porch, lit up with strings of star shaped bulbs across the ceiling, Aurora's heart ached for Logan's love. Instead of going inside to face him, she took off her boots and placed them next to his and found a comfortable seat on the rocking love seat hung with white coated chains from the ceiling. The evening breeze blew softly and the stars twinkled in the distant sky like the lights on the porch.

"Ready to come inside?" Logan asked softly.

The man was so quiet, she hadn't heard him open the door.

"It's a nice night. Want to join me on the porch?" *I'm not ready to face any remnants of Riley, yet.*

"Sure." He sat beside her on the love seat, raising his arm up over her and lowering it onto the back rest. "I missed you today."

"How's Riley?" *I don't want to talk about her, but she's all I can think about.*

"Better. She's got a lot of layers of abuse to peel back and get rid of; and with that comes a lot of temptation," he said. "She's a lot like your dad."

"Except she wants to get better. Dad chased the high. She's running from it."

"Exactly. I believe she'll get there with God's intervention through us." He slid her closer to him, until she was tucked in against his side. "We have to leave in the morning. The prosecutor called me this afternoon. The court date has changed again. The hearing starts tomorrow. There's no time to prep for your testimony."

"He's got the judge in his pocket and probably a majority of the jury." *Like he had every other time he was arrested for harassing and assaulting me.*

"He won't get away with it," Logan said. "The Georgia Law Angel is going to be there. I've been working with him. He just found out he is an angel and needs training to learn more about his full potential. He's going to be coming here to live with us in a couple months, so he will have not only me training him, but also my grandfather."

"Why is he living with us and not in the hotel or with Daniel?" *We're newlyweds. Who moves in with newlyweds? Is that normal for angels of the law? Will I have to go somewhere to learn about my skills?*

"I need to train him, which means he'll be with me all the time, except when sleeping. Uh, and he'll spend time with my grandfather, of course. Liam, the angel, has a lot to learn."

So, I've got to deal with Riley, who pretty much hates me, and a law angel who doesn't know anything about his job or skills or probably can't even keep his people safe. And he's in Georgia where the demon population is growing in the city.

She sighed. *I guess it won't hurt to have three angels of the law living in Exorcise. I'll need to have Daniel take me around to get what we need for Liam. I wonder if I should call Logan's grandfather by his first name while with Logan or not. I should ask. But first, I need to be supportive.* "We'll need to change the guest room around to accommodate Liam."

"He's not *living* in *our* house. He's living here, on our land, in a guest house that we need to build." He said it like it was no big deal to build a guest house in eight weeks.

"How can we build him a house in that short amount of time?" *Are you insane?*

"The construction builders and carpenters in the community will gather and help, but we'll design it and make it a home for him and others who might need us."

"He needs you, not me." *I have no skills. I don't know the rules. I have a lot to learn myself.*

"He does need you. He's been through a lot of trauma in his life and needs healing. Have some patience and trust your abilities." He lifted her onto his lap. "I love you, Aurora."

But you love Riley more. You love Riley, and you always will. "I need a little time alone out here."

"I know you heard me tell Riley that I loved her. I do love her, but I love her like I love my neighbors and the people who I protect."

"That's what Daniel explained while we were shopping today," she said.

"I love you in a very different way." He swept a handful of her blonde hair from her shoulder and raised it to his nose. He inhaled. "I love your citrus scent. I love your smile and laugh and moan. I really love to make you moan. I love your taste and your pure soul. I love the way you hold your tongue and think before you speak. I love you like I love no one else."

Instead of giving in and having him take her to bed like she wanted, she looked him in the eyes. "I love you, too. But I need to be outside for a bit. I need to breathe the country air, to gaze at the stars in the sky, to prepare to face the man who took my parents from me."

"Then we'll sit together," he said softly. "We can stay here all night, if you want."

She softened in his arms. "Thanks for staying with me." *Thanks for choosing me, tonight. I'll see if you continue to choose me, after you meet my demonic stalker.*

CHAPTER EIGHTEEN

Logan

Meeting the Georgia Law Angel Liam Hutchison Vogel outside the courthouse at the private entrance proved to make Aurora more comfortable. She hugged the man wearing a black SWAT uniform a little too long for Logan's liking. Her country drawl thickened when she spoke to him, and she blushed as she laughed at his jokes.

From the moment Aurora hugged Liam, the man took control, leading the way inside the new, beige-and-white brick building with an abundance of windows. He nodded at the other officers, stopping occasionally to introduce Logan and Aurora on the way to the courtroom. In the light-beige hallway, close to the room, he called to the prosecutors of the case and introduced Aurora.

Together, they all strode down the hall, passing lawyers, citizens, peace officers, families, and defendants.

Liam held open the door to the empty courtroom where Aurora would have to face the man she feared most. Her hand trembled, slightly, in his hand. She squeezed his hand and let go, but stepped closer to Logan. The prosecutors walked in first.

"Are you ready or do you want to walk the hall a little?" Logan asked. *You're keyed up and scared.*

"As long as you stay nearby, I'm ready." But her blue eyes flickered with glittering specks of gold, revealing to him that she was healing herself. Pain radiated off her in droves. The white cardigan over the sleeveless white dress with accents of yellow daffodils printed on the skirt that stopped a couple inches below her knees made her stand out from all the black and navy suits everyone else wore in the building. She stood like a vision of perfection at the threshold, next to Liam. The two angels so new to their roles—their real roles—in the battle of good versus evil had so much to learn.

Liam leaned toward her.

She stepped closer to him and tucked her wavy blonde hair behind her ear, using her fingers as a comb to pull more of it behind her and down to the middle of her back.

"You've proven you're brave," Liam said. "Now, tell the truth and what happens will happen. You are standing up to evil incarnate and showing that good will always prevail. Never back down. *Never* give up."

She inhaled and nodded. "I'll never give up. He might not pay for his crimes today, but I will tell the truth of what he did. People will know."

Leaving Liam at the entrance, she strode into the room

like a girl boss—in charge and powerful. Energy crackled in the air around her.

While Liam watched her, Logan stepped forward beside Liam.

"How corrupt are the people handling this case?" Logan asked.

Liam exhaled. "On a scale of one to ten. Ten being the most corrupt. We're looking at a twenty. The prosecution will do their best, but the judge is in the defendant's pocket. The jurors are scared of the defendant. But with you here, that number might drop substantially. The jurors might find some courage. But the photos of the scene were…horrific."

"Whatever happens today, doesn't matter as long as Aurora is protected. And after you've been trained, crime will decline in the state. There will be a small stronghold of evil, but you'll flush them out as your power grows." Logan strode forward, easily catching up with Aurora. With a gentle nudge on her back, he guided her to the middle chair in the first row behind the prosecution team. "You look beautiful, Mrs. Hutchison."

She lowered her chin and shook her head, but her skin flushed a pretty pink. "You look mighty handsome, Mr. Hutchison. I love you in that beige suit and cowboy hat." She sat down and Logan sat on the aisle chair.

Liam took the chair on the other side of Aurora and placed it closer to her. He leaned close to her. "Do not go anywhere in this building by yourself. Not even to the bathroom. Have your husband or me escort you inside any room you enter. Understand?"

"Yes, sir." She slipped her hand in Logan's and the

spark that was always there, under the surface, came forward. She pulled his hand into her lap.

"No matter what happens here, you are safe," Logan said. "I won't let anything happen to you." The energy in the room shifted. He stood up and turned toward the door to the exit.

White light with streaks of burnt orange and dark red moved through the gaps in the door and the holes in the locks.

No. You weren't supposed to have heard about my marriage or this court case. But you did. I shouldn't be surprised. You're on top of the world's food chain. You're the most powerful man in the world right now and you want to meet my wife. And you should want to meet her. I want you to meet her, but not now. Not here. Not until she's ready.

The door opened and Rager Smithson strode down the aisle wearing a black monochrome tuxedo and genuine grin. While he neared, he raised his arms for a hug. "Congratulations, my friend. I was going to wait, but since all the members of your church in Exorcise, Texas are allowed a visit immediately after the ceremony, I decided to come welcome the newlyweds, too. *This IS the church I found salvation in and claim as my own.* Although we're not in Texas. At least not at the moment."

Logan opened his arms, and the man's grin widened.

"Thank you for coming, Rager. But you could've waited until we got back home." *Not come to the courtroom. Although you're probably most comfortable in these surroundings.*

Logan hadn't intended to smile, but when Rager offered a genuine grin, he couldn't help but return it.

Rager walked forward and hugged him. "Brother, I've missed you."

Logan laughed. "Brother, I saw you a few days ago."

"I want you to move to Nevada," Rager said. "I'll build you a house in the neighborhood." He clung to Logan. "I truly missed you. Being away from you makes my everyday life a challenge that I don't enjoy."

The vulnerability in Rager's words struck Logan's heart as hard then as it had the first day Logan had met him. Very few people knew the man's internal struggles or external ones. Truly, Logan and his grandfather were the only ones walking the earth who Rager allowed to see into his soul. He rarely offered the gift of trust and with it came unconditional friendship and love. "I missed you, too. Come, meet my wife. I was going to—"

"I know you would've called or visited," he whispered. "But at the moment, sex and making babies is the only thing on your mind. I don't blame you. I'm close to my own wedding ceremony, and the path has been littered with road block after road block. I can't wait to get to the sex and possible babies with my future wife, but the things I'm doing to protect her..." He loosened his hold on Logan and stepped backward. He walked around Logan toward Aurora. "Mrs. Hutchison, I'm Rager Smithson, and I'm honored to meet you."

She stood and offered him her hand.

He took it and knelt on one knee, kissing her hand as though he were a knight kneeling before his queen. "A Lockhart and Vogel union of the utmost secrecy. I'll introduce you to your cousin, Wenzel Vogel, soon. Actually, it will be very soon. We'll keep the Lockhart side of your family a secret for now." He glanced at Liam. "You aren't to say a word about anything you hear from me today, not even to Wenzel. Do you understand, Mr. Liam Hutchison Vogel?"

Liam nodded. "Of course, Mr. Smithson." Liam stared at Aurora. "You're my cousin in blood and marriage."

"Yes, she is," Rager said. He bowed to Aurora, and then rose, releasing her hand. "You're a lucky woman to have Logan as a husband. He's the best man I've ever known, besides Wenzel." He glanced at Logan and laughed. "Wenzel brings the party with him."

"Wenzel parties too much," Logan said.

"All right, he's not the *best* man I've ever known. He's the most fun. Logan is the most pure, trustworthy, and faithful man I've ever known—but he lacks in the fun department." Rager's blue eyes sparkled with mirth. "So, tell me, Aurora, if you could have anything in this world, what would it be?"

"No, no," Logan said, stepping in front of his wife. "She doesn't need anything."

Rager's mouth clenched and his smile turned flat. "I *didn't ask you.* Move, Logan. I'm speaking with your wife, and you're being rude."

Logan took a step to the left and curled his arm around Aurora's waist, tucking her small frame against his side. "I apologize."

"So, what would you want, Aurora?" Rager's genuine smile appeared once more. "Jewelry, clothes, cars?" He tilted his head as he focused on her. "Private information? To hide your past? To know who your biological father really is?" He held his palms out to her. "Or…"

Aurora seemed drawn into Rager's world, walking forward and placing her small hands in his.

"Or," Rager started his inquisition again. "Aurora,

would you want vengeance? Would you want the murderer and his followers to finally pay for their crimes? They've done terrible things throughout their lives. What they did to your loved ones..."

The rise of powerful energy in Rager's spirit expanded and spread through the room, enveloping them. "They slowly destroyed your mother's spirit, making sure eternity in Heaven was lost to her. They sent the man you referred to as "Dad" straight to Hell. And if we're absolutely honest, your father deserved that sentence. He handed your mother to them on a silver platter. He offered her body, over and over, year after year. He offered *her soul* to save his own. He offered your hand in marriage to the piece of shit who will be in this courtroom, defending his actions to jurors he paid to vote in his favor. Your dad told of your virtue, of your purity, of ways to *turn you,* like they did your mother. He spoke secrets aloud that not only put you in danger, but others like you. He mentioned my friend's special ability —and he called my friend by name. If I were you—and to be clear, this is *not* my decision—I would seek vengeance. Do you want vengeance? Do you want the nightmares to end? Do you want those humans, who've called upon demons, to control cities through fear, through violence, through lies to continue their assault on good people?"

"I want so many things," she whispered.

No. Don't ask for a wedding gift. You have no idea the kind of Pandora's box your request will open.

"Tell me, Aurora Hutchison, what do you desire most, besides your husband?" Rager held her hands so gently, but ribbons of white and gold energy circled their hands as if their words were their bond—an unbreakable bond with consequences yet to be revealed

"What I want only God can give," she said. "And if it is God's will to give it to me, then I will have it one day."

"And that is the correct answer." Rager patted her hand. "I have your birthright—a birthright the man who tried to sell you to the highest bidder stole from you, when your biological father died. What you do with the ring, is up to you." He remained stationary as Logan's wife strode forward until she stood flush against him with her hands in his at her back.

A cloud moved into the room, blanketing them in a private embrace. When the cloud dissipated, Aurora wore a gold and diamond necklace with the Vogel insignia which dipped down between her breasts. The white dress with daffodils and matching white cardigan made the necklace pop, making her all the more beautiful and alluring.

"Thank you," Aurora said.

"Oh, it was my honor to return what was always yours," Rager said. "Now, I'd like to introduce you to Wenzel Vogel."

The doors to the courtroom burst open.

"Cousin!" Wenzel wearing a traditional black and white tuxedo strutted toward Aurora, smoothly skating by Logan and Rager. He picked Aurora up and spun her around in his arms while Aurora giggled. "Aurora Vogel. Sweet baby Aurora is now all grown up and married. Your father Egon would have been so proud of you. He loved you and your mother so much. You favor your mother, but you've got Egon's warrior spirit. You're a fighter."

Wenzel placed her down and then picked her up again

and hugged her. "I see you've met your cousin Liam Hutchison Vogel, and of course, there's Rager Smithson." He lowered his voice as if he were telling her a secret. "We call him *the Anointed One*. But really, he's just a pain in my ass." He placed her down. "At least you didn't marry him. Well, actually, that might've been better. Rager knows how to have a good time. The two boring ones on either side of us—I'm working on them, but they need some serious help in the fun department."

The giggles coming from Aurora's mouth sounded as innocent as a child's. And Wenzel ate them all up.

"I see you decided on boring," Wenzel teased. "Introduce me to Logan, not that I don't know him, but that is how these things are done."

"Mr. Vogel, this is my husband, Mr. Logan Hutchison." She held out her hand to Logan as he reached for hers, twining her fingers with his.

Logan tugged her hand and she stepped toward him. "Logan, meet Mr. Wenzel Vogel."

"Wenzel." Logan nodded.

"Logan," Wenzel mumbled. "It's a good match. Is your grandfather involved?" He raised his brows, and Aurora knew his question had everything to do with a triad relationship.

"No," Logan said. "Aurora and I are a perfect match. I don't share and neither does my grandfather."

"All the more reason to celebrate." Wenzel faced her and his eyes morphed to gold. "We have mandatory meetings once a month at my house. Logan is welcome to join us, since he will be the father of a Vogel child in nine months or so. All family is welcome, animals, too. We'll get you a jet to have at your disposal, and you'll stay in your father's house which happens to be within walking distance to my main home in Las Vegas. Actually, my house might not be within walking distance, but it's close. I'll send the keys to your new home. I've had our young herbalists keep up with his vast garden. His personal and gardening books are in his house, along with all his warrior gear."

"I'm a warrior angel?" Aurora asked.

"Oh, yes. And a healing herbalist. I officiated the marriage between your mother and father." Wenzel paused, seeming to have fallen into his memories. "Egon and I grew up like brothers. His death was…" He shook his head. "This is not the time to talk about the past. We will talk about the future. As a Vogel, regular rules apply —no telling others our secrets, or I'll kill you. And that will make me sad, which will make me unstable, and that's not good for anyone. So, let's avoid that by keeping our mouths shut about who and what we are. Got it?"

"Got it," she said.

"Did you kill her father?" The words came out of Logan's mouth before he could stop them, which was not like him at all.

"No," Wenzel said. "But that is a reasonable question. He passed away helping fight off demons on the outskirts of your territory. He and his brother perished honorably, in battle, and their spirits rose to the Heavens." He reached out and squeezed Aurora's arm. "I'm so sorry about your mom. I offered many times over the years to step in, but she turned me away, refusing my help. Rager Smithson and I flushed out those fuckers who scattered her spirit and latched her to a demon and took her to hell. Those demons wished they'd never dragged their nasty muck back to the surface…" He ground his teeth and the courthouse shook on its foundation.

"Was Slater with you?" Logan asked. *He's your second. He's your strategist. He's strong and brilliant and a warrior of unparalleled ability.*

"You know he was. Then we partied last night. Damn, we had a good time. We had a fucking great time. Anyway, I'm here. I'm claiming Aurora as my cousin later than I wanted, but it's all good, right?" He grinned and nodded and raised his hands in the air and swayed with whatever imaginary music was playing in his head.

"It is good that you're here," Aurora said, grinning just like him. "I can't wait to meet everyone, but I might have duties that interfere with family gatherings."

Wenzel took her hands, pulling her into his arms, and waltzed around the courtroom. "We'll figure it out, my sweet cousin." He continued waltzing and twirling her around until he brought her back to where they started and spun her into Logan's arms. "You're coming to my house this Friday. I'll take care of everything. Refusing isn't an option."

"I would never refuse you," Aurora blurted.

"That's right. We're family," Wenzel said. "Family is everything."

Aurora wrapped her arms around Logan's waist and hugged him. "Family is everything."

Wenzel grinned and danced out of the room, closing the door behind him.

Logan had seen Wenzel as a soldier, protector, fighter, warrior, and a partier, but this Wenzel was different. He moved through the courtroom without a care in the world. The energy lightened as if Aurora was in no danger at all. The man *danced and played* like nothing mattered…

"On that note, I'll take my leave," Rager said. "I'll see you soon." He nodded toward Aurora and followed a straight path toward the door, not looking back.

"What did you and Wenzel do?" Logan asked.

"No one threatens those we love, and that includes family by biology or by choice," Rager said. "Next time I send my plane for you, get on it and visit me."

"Oh, Rager. Was it a calling? Or was it Wenzel?"

"Logan, I only do what I'm called to do. No human on earth has authority over me. And neither do the angels."

"Thank you," Logan said. "Come to my house next week. Help us build a guest house. I need you, my brother in Christ."

He nodded. "I'll be there." He opened the door and exited the room.

"I loved both Wenzel and Rager," Aurora beamed. "I can't believe that this is all real. It doesn't seem real."

The gentle slap of closing laptops and the rustle of papers and the grinding sound of zippers alerted Logan to the prosecutors behind him. He pivoted, as the two-person team had turned into four while he and Aurora were having a meet and greet at the most inappropriate time. But the team had packed up their equipment and waited as Aurora slowly faced them.

"We just received disturbing news of a massive fire that happened overnight. More than twenty people were killed, including the defendant in this case. The bodies were identified by dental records. The case is now closed."

"He's gone, forever?" Aurora asked.

"Dead is as forever as it gets," the younger male prosecutor said. "The city is safer now that he's off the streets."

Aurora gazed at Logan. "He can't come after me?"

"Nope," Logan said. *Wenzel and Rager made sure of it.*

"I have a couple days off from work," Liam said. "Can I tag along to Exorcise with you? I'll help with the guest house and stay with your grandfather."

"Yes, you can." Aurora seemed to float on air as she led the way out of the courthouse.

Now, Rager and Wenzel and lots of Vogels will be in Exorcise before our plane touches down today. Not what I planned for today, but I'm sure Liam will have a home away from home to stay in today, furniture and all.

While Aurora continued leading the way outside, Liam strode by Logan's side.

"Aurora is still in danger, isn't she?" Liam whispered.

"She is," Logan answered. "She won't be leaving my territory without me, which means that she won't be able to attend all the Vogel mandatory meetings. We'll talk more about all the ins and outs of our laws, which are your laws."

"I'm in love with a girl. I think she might be part angel, but I'm not sure. What are the odds of me being able to marry her?"

"Depends on what kind of angel she is, if she is indeed an angel. Whatever she is, she will need to be able to live by all the rules that you live by, or face the consequences. Not all people, nor angels, are capable of our lifestyle." Logan expanded his aura, mixing his with Aurora's. "Have you spoken with Wenzel about your situation?"

"I have. He's going to look into it," Liam said. "But

Wenzel lives in his own world. Time means nothing to the man."

Aurora stopped in front of the passenger's side of the rental car. "If we hurry, maybe we can be home in time for dinner. I'm going to call your grandfather and ask him to pick up dinner for all of us. We can practice for the visitors who will be arriving at the house."

Logan opened her door. "That sounds like a wonderful idea. Call him and tell him the good news."

She climbed in and was on the phone before Logan closed her door.

While Liam slid into the backseat, Logan walked to the driver's side.

Demons are gathering in larger numbers. Angels are hiding their children.

A war is brewing.

I need to gather the other angels.

I need to prepare those I love.

I need to protect my people and my land.

I need to protect my wife.

EPILOGUE

Aurora

The flight to Texas on Wenzel's—now her—private plane with both Logan and Liam was some how smoother and much faster than the commercial flight to Georgia. Logan mumbled something about warrior angel pilots and their airstream antics, but she had no idea what he meant. She was just happy to be in Texas at lunch-time instead of dinner. But Logan grumbled about the schedule being changed without his approval. He grumbled even more when the pilots parked the plane in a private hangar at the airport. She didn't think that the name "VOGEL" stamped in polished gold throughout both the inside and outside of the building helped with Logan's mood.

Logan seemed less than pleased with the new gold-colored SUV with the license plates "AVOGEL" in front and back and a big golden bow on the hood with a card for her.

Logan grumbled, "Her name is Hutchison, not Vogel."

"I'll give it back," she whispered.

"No. You can't. It would be an insult," Logan said. "It's a nice vehicle. Wenzel loves giving his family gifts." He huffed, but seemed to calm down. "Open the card."

In her soul, the gift didn't feel like it was from Wenzel as much as it was from her biological father. The man she never met sounded like he would've been a wonderful father. She had no doubt that Wenzel had tried to intervene in her life, but her mother wouldn't allow him to help.

She opened the card.

Dear Aurora,

Enjoy the vehicle. Until I train you how to protect yourself, you'll have two warrior angels nearby to drive you anywhere you want to go without your husband. If he's unable to attend the mandatory meeting at my house in Las Vegas on Friday, they will bring you. YOU MUST ATTEND. No excuses. I've checked the rules for newlyweds and you will not break any rules by attending. We need you. We've been without a warrior-herbalist since your father rose to Heaven. There is much for you to learn and even more for me to show you.

Welcome to your warrior family,

~WVogel

LOGAN GRUNTED AND NODDED. "At least he checked the rules. That must be a first."

"And we're staying at Ranger and Malcolm Wenworth's house, while they're out of town, so that we remain within the rules of Exorcise, Texas," the two warrior angel pilots assigned to Aurora said in unison and then punched each other's chest and laughed. They pulled off the bow. "Hop in the backseat. This baby has some extra features that you're going to love, Aurora."

Between the warriors staying at the ranch next door and the drive with the driver pushing the speed limit to Logan's house, while explaining all the extra hidden features of the car, including seat ejectors and weapons on every surface within reach, Logan kept mumbling phrases like, "barely in the rules" and "loopholes are unacceptable," and every once in a while, "talking to Wenzel Vogel is like talking to a brick wall."

To make matters worse, the warriors rolled their eyes with every grumble Logan made and replied, "You're outnumbered here, Hutchison."

To which Logan repeatedly stated, "You wish."

The car slowed down and turned onto Logan's stretch of road and the colors in the sky shifted and sang praises to Heaven. White, light blue, burnt orange, red, deep forest green, and lavender rose and fell together like a musical score of pure harmony.

"You've got to be kidding me," Logan huffed.

"What's wrong?" Aurora asked. "The sky is beautiful. Do you hear the angelic music?"

"Yes, I hear it. Those are actual angels singing. It is beautiful. God is pleased, Aurora." Logan sighed and unbuckled Aurora's seatbelt, sliding her onto his lap. The irritation he'd had since Rager and Wenzel showed up in Georgia vanished with his next exhale. "I love you so much." He nuzzled his nose under her ear, leaving sweet kisses along her neck. "We have a lot of guests. Wenzel is here with many of his warrior angels. Rager is here working with the community on a guesthouse. And my grandfather is here working on a special project."

"Woah, Daniel is looking good," the driver—who Aurora still didn't know his or his partner's names—said. "I've never seen him in anything other than a suit, even when fighting."

The other man in the passenger seat pointed at Daniel. "You guys have your own merch?"

Logan kissed Aurora's cheek and looked at the man. "We're angels of the law. Of course, we have our own merchandise."

"Can I get a baseball hat like his?" Liam pointed to Daniel.

Logan nodded. "Yes. You're a Hutchison, you will be wearing the Hutchison brand, too. And that man is my grandfather Daniel Hutchison. He lives on a ranch nearby."

The car rounded the side of Logan's home—*her home.*

"Is that a new building near your workshop?" Aurora asked. "And is that a…Did Daniel prepare the soil and bring plants for my garden?"

"Mmm," Logan mumbled. "He spoke with Wenzel last night about making you a garden fit for a healing angel with a penchant for gardening. My grandfather loves you. He wants you to be as happy here as I am. As we all are. As God is."

"There's no crime here, is there?" Liam exhaled and his entire body relaxed.

"Nope," Logan said. He tipped his head to the left and opened the door. "Aurora, go to my grandfather and help him with your garden. Liam, follow her and do whatever my grandfather tells you to do." He stepped out onto the white gravel and strode up the gravel driveway toward the road.

Aurora hustled out of the car and ran to Daniel, while Liam followed, walking backwards, watching Logan.

Woah. Daniel has got a body on him, too. He looks even younger than he did the other day.

"Logan said to hang out with you and work on my garden," Aurora said. "Thank you for readying the soil and bringing so many herbs, flowers, and vegetables."

Daniel swiped the baseball hat off his head. All the silver in his hair was gone, leaving him with a thick mop of light brown hair. He looked younger, too. Not a wrinkle on his face and his body...If she didn't know better, she could easily mistake his body for Logan's. He curled his arm around Aurora's waist and tucked her against his side. "I'm going to open my wings. They won't hurt you." His head tipped to the left, just like Logan's had.

The music continued as everyone else worked, hammering nails, sawing wood, and hauling supplies from boxes on the grass into the first guesthouse they'd already built.

"What should I do?" Liam asked.

"Take off your gear and shirt and stay in front of me," Daniel stated.

The moment Liam stepped forward strobes of lights shone down from the sky, blinding her. Feathers as soft as silk caressed her ankles and legs, her neck and cheek, her hands.

She gazed up at the sky, and there, she saw the most magical sight. Logan flew across the sky, his wings growing in size. The tip of one of his brilliant white wings touched down to the ground.

Black smoke rose from the ground.

She couldn't look anymore and wrapped her arms around Daniel's waist, pressing her face against his chest and squeezed her eyes shut. "Please help him. Demons are coming. He's in danger."

"He's not in danger," Daniel cooed. "He's cut off entrance to our town to the demons coming for Riley and has extended the county line. He's following God's orders. Our wings are on display to show solidarity. We protect God's land and community." He curled his wing around her and pulled her closer to him. "Wenzel lives for a fight. Believe me, if he could get involved in this, he would. But this is an issue of law and the breaking of it, which is our department."

"We've added onto Logan and Aurora's home, built one guesthouse and have the bones of the other," Wenzel said. "And I added a sound system and an outdoor oasis for parties. Logan didn't have one. What kind of angel doesn't have a sound system for celebrations?"

Aurora remained inside Daniel's wing cocoon, but could hear conversations outside the cozy bubble Daniel kept her in.

"We have visits, not parties, Wenzel. You know this," Daniel said.

"That ends now. There is a Vogel living here. Egon danced, sang, and played music for his garden and those who helped tend it. He had planting and harvesting parties. My third in command—who is Aurora Vogel— will have the same. She may have to live here with you boring angels, but *she* will not succumb to your drab ways. Now, may I speak with Aurora, or are we going to fight it out?"

"You're being dramatic, Wenzel," Daniel stated.

"You're a little too comfortable with my first cousin, *Dan-iel*," Wenzel stated. "She's already healing you and she doesn't realize it. Soon, you and Logan will look like brothers. She might mistake you for him."

"You forget who you're talking to, my old friend," Daniel said. "We follow the law. We do not take what is not given to us by God. There may come a time where you might need to be in my place, Wenzel, protecting Aurora. Or your second Slater Vogel could be here, wrapping his wing around Aurora to protect her."

"Slater isn't interested in Aurora," Wenzel said. "He's not a fan of this place. Or to be more precise, he's not a fan of you."

"He broke the law," Daniel said.

"That's up for debate," Wenzel said.

"Regardless, he is always welcome here," Daniel said. "I look forward to seeing him again." His feathers brushed Aurora's hair and left feather kisses on her skin as his wing unfurled from around her. "Here she is, Wenzel. I'll help put the precious metal, Vogel stamped roof on the guest house your angels built on the south side of the ranch, which neither Logan nor I approved."

"It was approved by the Anointed One. I didn't need either of you to approve it."

"I'm aware," Daniel said. "But the courtesy of being told prior to breaking ground would've been nice."

"I'll keep that in mind for the next time. Oh, this is the next time. The border of Exorcise is being extended to the southwest. I'll be breaking ground on Aurora's healing clinic for angels on my next visit. Actually, Rager and I will be building it together."

"Thank you for telling me," Daniel said. "God already spoke to me about Aurora's needs and I extended the county in the south and west yesterday. This morning, I prepared the building of the clinic and a small home for Aurora's helpers. I do hope that Slater chooses to come for a visit. He will need us, soon."

"I doubt it," Wenzel mumbled.

Daniel kissed the top of her head. "Logan finished with the lawbreakers, but will be dealing with Riley until late this evening." He put on his baseball cap and strode toward Liam.

Wenzel grabbed her hand and walked up the gravel drive to the road. In an instant she was enclosed with Wenzel in his wings. "This is a private conversation that needs to stay between you and me for now. I left two books on healing in the top dresser drawer. One is for a healing angel, like you but without the warrior and herbal remedy abilities. The other is for a love angel. I think we might be looking at a hybrid who isn't aware she's an angel. Liam needs healing, too. When he comes for training, Logan and Daniel will help him heal his spirit, but he will need help with his mind and body. I'll give you the rest of what you need as your gifts expand."

"Can I read it at night in front of Logan?" she asked.

"Yes. And you should always obey him over me, but when I call you to come, I expect you to be there, even if it is with Daniel—the master of boring. Logan knows I will never call into question his rule of law, and he knows that your ranking in my family is too high for you to ignore my call. Egon was my uncle, so you are my first cousin. You're his only child. Have your wings appeared, yet?"

"I have wings?" she asked.

"You will. They'll start out as delicate butterfly-like wings, but they will be a translucent gold. After a few years, they'll drop and you'll sprout wings like mine. The other side of your family, the Lockhart angels don't have wings. I'll tell you more about them each time we talk. I love you and I will teach you as much as I know about herbs and Egon as I'm able."

"Thank you, Wenzel. I think that Logan will be at the meeting with me on Friday."

"Let me know when your first wings appear. We will need to celebrate."

"I will," she said.

The feather enclosure vanished in an instant.

"Let's get back to work," Wenzel said. "I need to mark off a placement for an outdoor dance floor, bar, and gazebo before Logan gets back or he'll try and stop me." He nodded at her, and a flash of bright white light blinded her for a second.

When her eyes adjusted, golden wings expanded so large, she couldn't see her house or anything in front of her. With a flap of his wings, he rose into the air and in another flap, a gold streak of light raced across the sky and dropped out of sight.

I have two wonderful families. I have a career as a healer. I'm going to have wings. REAL WINGS. Best of all, I have a husband who loves me and place to call home.

The End 💋

Want to read more about more angels? Read the next story in the Fallen Angels and Demon series...*Fallen Angel: Slater*

Also, thank you so much for reading Logan and Aurora's story. If you loved it, please rate/review this book. Your rating/review helps indie authors more than you know!

For more steamy stories and to join Anna's VIP Lounge, visit
https://www.AnnaLoresAuthor.com

ABOUT THE AUTHOR

An avid romance reader, Anna Lores started writing steamy romance novels as a by-product of insomnia. One night, with a nudge from her husband to write a book, Anna borrowed her son's laptop and set about breathing life to her very own characters. After a month, she was surprised with a new laptop of her own to pursue her dreams of writing sensual happily ever afters.

The desire to fill her world with wonderful stories she and her close friends could not just talk about but gush over keeps Anna's fingers racing to keep up with her imagination. As the rest of the house is sleeping peacefully, Anna sheds her title as Supermom of Three to write sexy love stories

Sleeping might still be a battle Anna hasn't conquered, but armed with a B. A. in English Literature and all the hot men in her mind calling for their own story, she stays busy during those midnight hours writing her next international bestselling spicy romance.

Visit http://www.AnnaLoresAuthor.com/ for more information and to sign up for Anna's VIP Newsletter.

facebook.com/AuthorAnnaLores

bookbub.com/authors/anna-lores

x.com/AnnaLores

instagram.com/AnnaLoresAuthor

goodreads.com/annalores